I0521376

Author of *Voice from the Shadows* and *Night Journey*

H. Scott Butler

A Cynthia Westbrook Mystery

Falcon

Copyright © 2017 H. Scott Butler

All rights reserved.

No part of this publication may be reproduced, distributed or transmitted in any form or by any means, including photocopying, recording, or other electronic or mechanical methods, without the prior written permission of the publisher, except in the case of brief quotations embodied in critical reviews and certain other noncommercial uses permitted by copyright law.

For permission requests, write to the publisher, addressed "Attention: Permissions Coordinator," at the address below.

High Tide Publications, Inc.

1000 Bland Point Road

Deltaville, Virginia 23043

www.HighTidePublications.com

Edited by: Narielle Living (NarielleLiving@gmail.com)

Cover by: Firebelliedfrog@gmail.com

Printed in the United States of America

ISBN-13: 978-1945990038

Publisher's Note: This is a work of fiction. Names, characters, businesses, places, events and incidents are either the products of the author's imagination or used in a fictitious manner. Locales and public names are used for atmospheric purposes. Any resemblance to actual persons, living or dead, or to businesses, companies, institutions, actual events or locales is purely coincidental.

Publisher's Note:

Falcon is Scott's third book in the *Cynthia Westbrook Mystery* series. We have included bonus material in this first edition - chapter one from both *Night Journey* (his first book) and *Voice from the Shadows*.

Here are a few comments from readers about Scott's work. We are proud to represent him, and hope you enjoy the additional chapters in the back of this volume.

Voice from the Shadows by H. Scott Butler

By Jennifer Britt,

Chesapeake Style magazine, Spring 2015

It has been a long time since I've read a book from cover to cover in one sitting, but Voice from the Shadows made for a very pleasant morning. Like all good mysteries, it is not only a satisfying who-done-it, but a compelling journey of self discovery.Cynthia Westbrook, an investigator with a sheri 's department in Virginia, returns to her childhood home in Alabama to solve a 24 year old cold case—the murder of her mother. In so doing, she confronts the horrors of a past that she has spent her adult life repressing. Armed with nothing more than details gleaned from a few newspaper articles and even fewer surviving witnesses, she manages to tease the truth from between the lines and provoke a serial killer into showing himself, with fatal consequences. The story's prose is intelligent, uncluttered and, sometimes, breathtaking. No need for Christie's red herrings or Evanovitch's sly humor. Butler gives the reader an elegantly devised plot with literary allusions that illuminate the protagonist's inner reality and provides us with an ending that is more than a reassuring triumph of good over evil...it is a poignant musing on the nature of memory, love and immortality. The book is available at Barnes and Noble, www.amazon.com and from the author at: http://hscottbutler.comScott Butler earned a doctorate in English from Duke University and taught literature and film at a community college in eastern Virginia for many years. He currently lives with his wife in Newport News, Virginia and spends much of his spare time participating in a grassroots effort to preserve Fort Monroe, a former Army post of deep historical significance

HRBooks Review | "Night Journey" by H.Scott Butler

By Tim Lee, #HRBooks contributor

(Hampton Roads Daily Press, May 20, 2015)

Three essentials transform the crime genre into absolute literature: Noncomformist cops, unimaginable evil and an unexpected locale. H.Scott Butler's "Night Journey" expertly incorporates these criteria.

Campell County Sheriff's investigator (much more likely to encounter sheriffs than dectectives out here in the country) Cynthia Westbrook is six-two, and her gender is still a novelty, as well as is her African-American partner, Jeff White. Neither receives respect from area law enforcement.

A third abduction in their territory launches "Night Journey" into an accelerated, authentic police procedural. The setting is no gritty urban street. Campbell County is Northern Virginia horse country.

Having lived in Warrenton, Virginia for two years, I can appreciate Butler's take on small-town life nestled amid wealthy owners and their equestrian pride. The working class travel in quiet communities amid stone mansions, rugged mountainsides and undeveloped expanses where beautiful stallions and mares run.

Investigating crime in her own neighborhood—opening doors and exhuming secrets where her heart has always been—is unsettling for Westbrook. Perfectly pragmatic, she pulls thread after thread on an evolvingly arduous case.

Other lawmen appear from Baltimore and Quantico, but this remains Westbrook's affair, and she can count on only White and her intuition.

Butler's descriptive flair draws in a huge breath of countryside: "...the ruinous house looked vaguely like a head...posts resembled crooked teeth...vines a dark,ragged mustache and the roof a battered hat pulled down over the eyes." One can just hear the cicadas and smell mustard greens cooking.

I am reminded of the top selling blockbusters "Gone Girl" and "The Girl on the Train" where powerful female characters have led the suspense novel scene of late. Perhaps most striking is the contrast between the interspersed chapters of history and psychotic justification from a monster, and Westbrook's heartbreaking empathy.

Something prevails in the end that will make you appreciate every word of this book.

Newport News author shines in second novel

Tim Lee#HRBooks contributor

Good works are written faster than I can turn the pages, and H.Scott Butler's "Voice from the Shadows" is in its second year. But classic storytelling ages well and the latest Cynthia Westbrook mystery is a captivating and scary slice of crime drama.Westbrook ventures home to find the man who murdered her mother and then chased 9-year-old Cynthia into the woods, whose cover saved her life, but also kept her lost without food or water for two days. It's no wonder this has become her recurring nightmare and she intends to bring the boogeyman to justice.She is a skilled detective who captured a serial killer in Virginia, but that feat has made her a reluctant celebrity. And no training or experience can soften the painful scars opened on a 30-year-old crime.Butler does his genre proud, as adept at no-one-is-as-they-seem plotlines as anyone I've ever read. His character profile and dialogue offer the realism of the best contemporary novels. It doesn't get more real than going home, especially in a country town where everyone knows your origin and your family tree. Nothing could be more emotionally punishing than having a mother murdered young and an absent father. The only family reunion will be at a grave siteBut Westbrook didn't make Sheriff's Detective without getting results, and she is strong enough to keep some personal issues aside for the largest one of all. She learns her mother's boyfriend, and chief suspect in her death, has righted his irresponsible ways with his new family.I tried to glean the obvious culprit from the cast of usual suspects — but how do you scrutinize everyone mentioned, those seen, unseen, mentioned and barely alluded to?I failed, which I'm grateful for, for what is a mystery spent too early? Not this readable.Resolutions come, and like the works of Tony Hillerman and other master writers, the revelations unfold in a nice flow of occurrence. The value of not only a crime solved but other pressing human issues cannot be underestimated.And gotta say, I'm quite taken by the image of a 6-foot-2 female cop who loves books. Butler has devoted his retired life to writing and preserving Fort Monroe, which makes him a fine author and a good citizen. He has a doctorate in English from Duke University and lives in Newport News with his wife Susan. "Voice from the Shadows" can be found for $14.99 on amazon.com in paperback.Lee, a former staffer for East Coast pop culture magazine Catharsis, lives in Newport News.Copyright © 2017, Daily Press

As always, for Susan and Anne

Turning and Turning in the widening gyre
The falcon cannot hear the falconer;
Things fall apart; the centre cannot hold;
Mere anarchy is loosed upon the world.

—W. B. Yeats, "The Second Coming"

Chapter 1

MIKE FALLON SAT DOWN BEHIND the glass, which was a little smeary from palms pressing against it on both sides. When they picked up their phones, he said, "Good to see you, Cynthia," and she said, "Hi, Mike." Their exchange of greetings was also a test of the phones. Sometimes these didn't work, and they'd have to shout at each other. Down the way, at one of the other booths, someone was shouting, but it was only the loudest sound in a rumble of voices, some full of anger or recrimination, issuing from the mouths of wives and mothers and girlfriends, and from the other side too. She put her hand over her free ear to muffle the noise.

Fallon had grown a beard since she'd last seen him a month ago. Shaggy and mostly gray, it made him look like one of those street-corner preachers prophesying the end to indifferent passersby.

"Why the beard?" she said.

He shrugged. "Got tired of shaving."

Something else about his face was different, too. Above the beard his cheekbones seemed sharper. She glanced at what was visible of his jump-suited torso on the other side of the booth. He was a large man, broad-shouldered and bulky, who could lose a few pounds without showing it, but she thought she detected some shrinkage.

"You doing okay?" she said.

He shrugged again. "How's the new home situation working out?"

"Good," she said. "Jack didn't have much he wanted to bring with him, and I was mostly interested in moving my books, so there wasn't any problem combining our stuff. And where we are, we don't even need an alarm clock. The birds wake us up."

It was a kind of game they played. She'd ask him about himself, and he'd deflect. A year and a half ago, following a hunch, she'd tracked him to Maryland and arrested him at the scene of the torture-murder he'd just committed, in revenge for his niece's death. The crime had repulsed her, but the victim, a serial killer she'd been seeking in her Virginia county, had planned to kill her, and might have succeeded if Fallon hadn't captured him first. Also, Fallon was a retired Baltimore cop who'd once taken a bullet to save a woman from her ex-husband. For these reasons, she'd been unable to forget him, and about a year ago she'd driven up to the Hagerstown prison where he was incarcerated. She hadn't known what to expect, but he'd seemed grateful for the company and they'd talked easily enough, with him directing the conversation to her life.

"Jack have any clients yet?" he said.

"Full slate. There seem to be a lot of children in need of therapy. I was worried he'd find private practice as hard, in some ways, as his old FBI job studying terrorists and so on"—the *so on* encompassing murderers like Fallon—"but I think he's thriving. He sees it as a chance, he says, to make things better instead of just picking through the wreckage."

Fallon nodded. "What about you? Things better with the new boss?"

"Well, temperamentally he's an improvement over Sampson. But Sampson still keeps his hand in as sheriff." She glanced at Fallon's sharp cheekbones again. "You look like you've lost some weight."

"Thanks, by the way, for that book of poems," he said, ignoring her observation. "I actually liked some of them. Surprised myself."

It was the other thing they did. She brought him books, and they talked about them. He hadn't been much of a reader in his previous life, so she'd started him off with writers he had some acquaintance with, Hemingway and Steinbeck (she'd also thrown in a John McDonald, but he told her he couldn't read "crime stuff," it was too unrealistic). Then she'd brought him some Conrad and Hardy, and Faulkner's *The Bear*, and last month she'd given him a thick paperback anthology of modern poetry.

"Which ones did you like?" she said.

"The Robert Frost one about the hired man; and a short one about eating up all the plums in the fridge."

"William Carlos Williams."

"Yeah. But my favorite is by that Irish guy, Yeats, about things falling apart."

"The Second Coming." It had crossed her mind more than once in recent years. *Mere anarchy is loosed upon the world.* Terrorists blowing people up, beheading journalists, stabbing artists. In this country, a homegrown epidemic of mass murders. The internet fizzing with hate. And following Obama's election, the resurgence of militias and white supremacist groups. *The best lack all conviction, while the worst/Are full of passionate intensity.* The best might not be feckless, but the worst were surely passionate. She wondered how Fallon saw himself in relation to the violence, since his hands were bloody too—they had been, literally, when she arrested him.

"I get at the beginning," he said, "that the falconer's lost control of the falcon. But what's that have to do with Bethlehem at the end?"

"Yeats thought history occurred in two-thousand-year cycles, and a more violent cycle was beginning."

"Sounds about right."

His small eyes, suddenly fragile-looking, fixed on hers, and another line from the poem popped into her head: *Surely some revelation is at hand.*

"Had some pain a few weeks back," he said, "and they diagnosed me with prostate cancer."

The way he said it, it sounded like a death sentence. But she asked, "You getting treatment for it?"

"Too late for that. It had already spread here and there. They gave me a year, but I figure that's a stretch."

She saw him anew. He was beginning to waste away, and something in his expression, a lack of tension, suggested he was on pain medication. "I'm sorry, Mike," she said.

"Don't be. Better than this."

Knowing he had no family except his dead niece's aunt and uncle, she said, "Have you told the Bradfords?"

He shook his head. "No point. They never thought much of me in the first place, and after…" He smiled. "Anyway, the good news is, the state might not get all my money. You have to pay for your room and board here—and medical treatment too."

She nodded. "Same in Virginia, in most states now. Terrible idea."

"Yeah, well. If there's anything left, maybe you could use it to buy yourself a few more books."

Reflexively, she said, "Oh, no, I couldn't—I mean, you'd do more good giving it to a charity."

He nodded, and she saw in his eyes the recognition of her recoil. "Okay," he said. "It was just an idea."

"Maybe I could help you decide on where…" she faltered.

"Sure. How's your detective partner, by the way? He coping okay with being a daddy?"

Grateful for the change of subject, she talked about Jeff, who'd married last year and recently become a doting father. And then a voice said in the phone, "Two minutes," and it was time to go. She started to ask if she could do anything for him, but he'd already told her and she'd turned him down.

"I'll see you soon," she said.

"I'll be here," he said, "unless I'm not."

Chapter 2

ON THE DRIVE BACK, PASSING through the freshly green countryside on a perfect spring day, she contended with both sadness and regret. Mike's news had affected her more than she might have guessed, and her rejection of his magnanimous gesture filled her with guilt—and shame. It was distressing to realize that beneath her supposedly good intentions lay a bedrock of harsh judgment.

She stopped in Parkerville to buy a bottle of wine for dinner tonight at Sally's, and, leaving the downtown, successfully resisted the urge to turn in the direction of her old apartment. She was getting better at it, after three weeks of living with Jack. The new way took her over a railroad track and down a country lane past a couple of trailers to the little house they were renting, with meadow on either side and woods close behind. She found Jack at the kitchen table reading the paper and drinking coffee. He looked up at her over the tops of his reading glasses.

"What's that good smell?" she said, kissing him on the cheek.

"Cherry pie, for Sally. Almost done."

One of the things about him she hadn't known before they moved in together was that he'd been the family chef. His ex-wife, who otherwise didn't communicate with him, occasionally texted him requesting recipes. His culinary skills were a pleasant surprise. Though Cynthia liked good food, she wasn't interested in preparing it herself and had subsisted on frozen and canned stuff in between the Mexican extravaganzas at Sally's, prepared by Sally's cook Maria. But no more. Most evenings when she got home Jack had a tasty meal waiting for her. She hadn't eaten this well on a regular basis since her late teens when she'd lived in the cabin on Sally's horse farm with Bill, the elderly, elfin African-American manager, who'd made the best fried chicken and cornbread and mustard greens she'd ever had. As a result of Jack's cooking, she'd put on a few pounds, much to the delight of Maria, who'd been trying to fatten her up for years. "You filling out so good," Maria liked to tell her now. "You no eskinny like them models."

She said to Jack, "You can bake a cherry pie, you're the apple of my eye."

He smiled. "But I'm not a young thing."

"Well, that suits me, since I'm past my prime."

His smile grew a little rigid. It was her running joke, but it still made him uncomfortable. They'd first met at Quantico, where as a forensic psychologist he'd advised her on the serial-murderer case and said in the process—a remark that turned out to be prescient—that she seemed more the killer's type than Fallon's missing niece. But unfortunately for him, he'd already described the other victims as slightly past their prime.

"How was your visit with Mike?" he said.

"Bad news. He has prostate cancer, and it's metastasized. Nothing they can do, he said."

Jack mulled over this information. He was looking at it, she knew, from various angles, trying to determine how he could be most helpful. It was his habit of mind, and heart.

"How's he taking it?" he said.

"Like a tough cop. He also said it was better than prison, and I think he meant it."

"And how are you taking it?"

"I don't know. I—" She stopped herself.

He waited for her to continue.

"He wanted to leave me his savings, and I refused. I wasn't very gracious about it, either."

"How'd he react?"

"Unlike me, he was tactful—he changed the subject."

"Because he appreciates you. Still appreciates you."

Not for the first time, she thought how nice it was to come home to Jack. He hadn't dispelled her guilt, but he'd given her some hope, at least, she could make it up to Fallon. "How was your day?" she said.

"Good." He elaborated in the general, circumspect way he did, not naming names. A borderline anorexic had gained a few pounds, a child with OCD was responding well to the combination of Jack's therapy and the medication prescribed by a psychiatrist.

The magnetic dinger on the fridge sounded.

"That's my pie," he said.

Using potholders, he took the pie from the oven and placed it on a rack on the table. She watched him performing this simple task, his errant lock of hair overhanging his forehead, and his sharp, somewhat villainous features blank with concentration. It was a common expression of his. He was given to introspective silences. She gathered this had had an alienating effect on his ex-wife, but she didn't mind it. Silence was her element too. She'd lived alone for more than a decade before Jack, and kept to herself for many years before that, going back to her mother's murder when she was nine.

"Want some coffee?" he said.

And while the pie cooled, they sat quietly and drank their coffee.

❀ ❀ ❀

Sally's farm, twenty miles south of Parkerville at the bottom of the county, was a hundred acres of rolling meadow traversed by a brook and backed by verdant mountains. At any given time there might be twenty or so horses scattered across the terrain, grazing or standing like statues and thinking their horsy thoughts, which she imagined as like the clouds drifting above them, formless and unhurried. She loved riding horses and grooming them and watching them, though her work pretty much limited her to the last activity. Taking care of them had been her first job. Sally had picked her up hitchhiking when she was a runaway from a foster group home and given her the job and a place to stay, and in her cabin-mate Bill, who'd had final approval on this arrangement, a teacher and a mentor.

Turning into the long drive, she felt a little rush of happiness. Although she hadn't admitted it to herself for many years, the farm was home. She was like Frost's hired man in that respect, feeling this was the one place where she belonged, to which she could always return. The house itself looked nothing like a farm house. It was a flat-roofed, longish structure with a courtyard entrance in the middle and plenty of glass in the back. Sally had torn down the too-far-gone original dwelling and put this one in its place, using her substantial divorce-settlement money to build just what she wanted. Cynthia parked in the circular drive and they went in through the always unlocked front door, Jack strumming the wind chimes to announce them.

Sally appeared at the end of the short hall, wearing her usual outfit of jeans and t-shirt, her white hair cut in a sort of Dorothy Parker bob. In her 80s now, she was a bit stooped but otherwise vigorous seeming. She met them halfway and gave Cynthia a strong hug and a kiss on the cheek, and the same for Jack.

"How are my two favorite people?" she said.

Fine, they told her, and Jack added, "How are you? Still having that back pain?" It was something he'd spotted the last time they were here, from the way Sally got out of her chair, and he'd forced her to confess to it.

She dismissed the pain with a wave of her hand. "Comes and goes. Mostly I don't notice it."

"So you haven't been to a doctor about it?"

"What's in your bag?" Sally said, changing the subject. It occurred to Cynthia that Sally and Mike Fallon might have hit it off, under other circumstances.

"Cherry pie," said Jack.

"Oh, goody. My favorite, as you know. Come in!"

They followed her into the kitchen, and while she put Maria's dishes in the oven to warm, Cynthia opened the wine and poured the glasses. Then they took their drinks into the den, where Sally, something of a political junkie, switched on the TV to catch the latest on the Senate race. Tim Kaine, a former governor, and the only Democratic candidate, was shown talking to a reporter. "I wish he could stop cocking that eyebrow," said Sally, who took a sort of handicapper's interest in the race. The Kaine piece was followed by a brief survey of the Republican contenders, the chief ones being George Allen, another former governor, and Jim Gates, a retired Marine general. When Gates appeared, straight-backed and silver-haired and craggy, visiting a veterans' hospital with his wife and daughter, Sally said, "Now that's what a general should look like."

She was not impressed, however, by the other Republicans running, and in particular Sam Spencer, a thirty-something state senator and Roanoke businessman. Spencer passed Sally's eye test; he was long and lean, with big, dark eyes and a square jaw. But he was ill-mannered, even to the extent of mocking the competition. He called Allen "the cowpoke" because of Allen's penchant for wearing a cowboy hat and boots, and he referred to Gates, the leader in the polls, as General Jellyfish for taking a nuanced approach to certain issues dear to conservatives. As Cynthia watched a clip of Spencer at one of his rallies leading a chant of "Take America Back!", his campaign slogan, she thought again of the line from Yeats's poem about the worst being full of passionate intensity. Spencer struck her as an embodiment, or a manipulator, of the dark emotions unleashed upon the world.

After dinner, they returned to the den, and Cynthia walked over to the picture window that looked out on meadow and hillside and mountains, all bathed in violet evening light. She peered at the little hilltop cemetery—visible chiefly because of its wrought-iron fence—that had come with the property and was now Bill's resting place. Looking at it usually stirred memories of Bill, but this evening Mike Fallon intruded upon her meditation. Sally, whose only child had died long ago, had insisted on leaving Cynthia everything, an offer she hadn't been so tactless as to refuse, and she couldn't help thinking that someday she'd be gazing out at both Bill's and Sally's graves. Of course, life didn't necessarily conform to the general pattern. She could go first, or Sally could live to be a hundred and ten, both comforting thoughts in a way, if you didn't pursue them too far. But the likelihood was she'd survive her friend, and Fallon's illness gave it more weight. Suddenly, the life she had now, the good life, felt imperiled, with the egregious Sam Spencer somehow adding to the sense of threat. It was as if everything had been moving incrementally toward a tipping point, and now they were there.

Jack joined her at the window, not saying anything. She put her arm around him and they watched the outer light fade. When they sat back down with Sally, the window had become a mirror, showing them as ghosts in a ghostly room.

Chapter 3

"HEY," THE CALLER SAID. "STEVE WILLIAMS, North Hill police? Don't know if you remember me, but—"

"I remember," she interrupted. Hard to forget the young cop with whom she'd had a one-night dalliance, following a fight with Jack during their early days. Or to be fair to Jack, not so much a fight as her anger at him for offering some unsolicited advice about her difficulty sleeping—advice she'd ended up taking, to her benefit.

"I was wondering," Williams said, "if you could spare me an afternoon to check out a situation. I'd appreciate your perspective on it."

"What situation?"

"There's a guy who's taken in some transient types, a man and a woman, and his neighbor's worried they might have taken him in."

"Who's the guy?"

"Henry Arnold. Wealthy, or his parents were—they're both dead. He lives in their house. He's kind of an oddball, from what the neighbor said."

"How so?"

"Keeps to himself, no job."

"Yet he's invited some strangers in. What do you know about them?"

"Not much," Williams said. "The neighbor, who was a friend of the mother, says she saw Arnold with them a couple of weeks ago protesting outside the abortion clinic in North Hill."

"The North Hill Medical Center for Women."

"Right."

"It isn't just for abortions," she said.

"I know, but that's the reason for the protesters. Or the main reason. Some of them might object to birth control too—though it helps their cause. Anyway, the neighbor didn't think Arnold was into that kind of thing before, and then she happened to see him turning into his drive with these people in the car. She was concerned, or nosey, depending on your point of view, so she dropped in on him, and found out they're staying there. I got Arnold's picture from his driver's license and swung by the clinic yesterday and eyeballed the three of them. The guy is middle-aged, like Arnold. The woman is young and looks to be pregnant."

"Any thought on her relationship to the man?"

"Well, he's old enough to be her father, but I'm guessing husband."

"Okay, I'm in." Actually, she was in from his first comment on the people. She hadn't shaken her gloomy mood from the night before, and this might help. "When do you want to do it?"

"I drove back by the clinic around two, and they were gone. So I'm thinking maybe we could catch them some afternoon at Arnold's house. Be a better place to talk than downtown."

"How about this afternoon? I'm good, so far."

"Sure."

After lunch, which she had with her partner Jeff down the street from headquarters, examining with unfeigned interest his latest cell-phone photos of Angela, his baby daughter, she drove to the North Hill station, flashed her badge, and went through to the main room. Williams, who was at a desk, gave her a big smile. He was as good looking as ever, or more so. Since she'd last seen him, he'd filled out a little in the chest and shoulders, though not in the waistline, and he'd let his dark curly hair grow a bit longer.

"You lost the pony tail," he said, apparently doing a similar reconnaissance of her.

"Got tired of it swishing around when I jogged."

He gestured at the side chair. "I like it. Frames your face."

Sitting down, she wondered if he was interested in more than her assistance.

"A little bird told me you'd moved in with some shrink," he said.

"That little bird is accurate, for once. What about you—still playing the field?"

He grinned at her. "Is that what you think of me?"

"Uh huh."

"In that case, sorry to disappoint, but I'm getting married."

"Oh? Who to?"

"Her name's Shannon, Shannon Boyd. She's in security at the college. Reminds me a little of you, in fact. Feisty."

"Feisty?"

"Is that not politically correct?" he said. "How about *independent?*"

"Better. And congratulations. I'm impressed."

"Thanks. We're thinking, or Shannon is thinking, late summer for the wedding. You're invited, of course. What about you and the shrink—any wedding plans?"

She shook her head. "Not that far along."

"Now look who the serious one is."

"Touché," she said, and glanced at her watch. "It's after two.

Maybe we should go by the clinic and see if Arnold and his friends have left."

Williams ushered her out to his cruiser and drove them to the clinic on the west end of town.

"Gone," he said as they crawled past it.

But there were plenty of other people. She estimated thirty or so, the majority of them men. They took up both sides of the walk, creating a gauntlet. Some were sitting in lawn chairs, but most were standing, and nearly everyone had a sign. One of signs said *Rape and Abortion are Wrong*. An equivalency, she supposed, meant to discourage impregnated rape victims from easing their ordeal.

Williams pointed to a little cluster of gray-haired men. "See the cardboard box on the ground next to those guys?" he said. "When a woman's going in, they dump it out in front of her. It's full of baby-doll parts spattered with red paint."

"She could be going in for something else."

"Doesn't matter to them." He turned north toward the countryside. "Arnold's male guest, by the way, was carrying a sign that said *Go And Sin No More*."

"What Jesus says to the adulteress."

"I thought it sounded familiar. She the one about to be stoned?"

"Right. But her accusers don't go through with it because Jesus says to them, *He that is without sin—*"

"*Let him cast the first stone,*" Williams finished for her.

"And then they slink away."

"Hard to imagine anybody reacting like that today. Lots of self-righteousness, not much shame."

She glanced at Williams, who continued to surprise her.

"But wouldn't the message be kind of sympathetic to the women going in?" he asked.

"I suppose," she said. "If they change their minds. Our young woman—I wonder if she isn't a kind of sign herself."

"You mean being pregnant, she's like an example of what other women should do?"

"By some people's lights."

"Lotta people."

She didn't know whether this was an endorsement of the anti-abortion movement, or simply an observation. But she decided not to pursue it. Abortion had to be a woman's decision, in her opinion, because it was so personal. The law couldn't encompass and morally parse all the circumstances in a pregnancy. Also, right-to-lifers tended to be absolutists who, if they got the chance, wouldn't allow exceptions even for incest and rape. Like Sam Spencer. But beyond these considerations, the idea of abortion made her uneasy.

They were in the upscale countryside now, passing big houses—chateaus, Italian villas, Tudors, every sort of wealth display—well set back from the road and separated from one another by fenced meadows, in which grazing horses could sometimes be glimpsed. The occupants were lawyers and lobbyists and other professionals who worked, or had worked, in D.C., having been drawn there like bugs to a street lamp.

"If Arnold's house is one of these," she said, "his inheritance was probably substantial."

"Yeah, I imagine so. An old cop told me Arnold's dad was a developer in the D.C. area—hotels and office buildings. He—the dad—died about twenty years ago in the crash of his private plane. There was a young woman with him who was killed too."

"Ah," she said. "What about the mother?"

"She died maybe four years ago. I actually met her once. Wrote her a ticket for running a stop sign. Attractive woman for her age, but cold as ice. She didn't say a word or even look at me. And the ticket went away."

"Friends in high places."

"Also, just to be thorough, I checked to see if Arnold has a record, and he does. Arrested last year in a John sting at an Arlington hotel. He paid a fine."

Williams slowed and turned into a drive flanked by stone pillars and hedges. The drive took them down a forested hillside to a huge gray-stone Georgian with towering opposed chimneys and a sliver of pond or lake shimmering to one side behind it. The lawn, long overdue for a mowing, was overrun by dandelions, and the ornamental shrubs had reverted to their natural bushy shapes.

"The neighbor told me about the yard," Williams said. "I think it disturbed her as much as anything."

At the center of a circular driveway was a circular, stone-bordered flower garden that had also seen better days, with only a few blooms visible among the sprawling weeds. And when they parked, she saw that the paint was flaking on the house's white portico and numerous black shutters. Arnold was either low on money or didn't like having people around to do the maintenance. But if it was the latter, he'd evidently made an exception for his guests.

"Maybe one of us should get Arnold off by himself," Williams said.

"Good idea," she said. "Why don't you take him? I'd like a shot at the guests."

Arnold met them at the door. Cynthia figured it was him, given what Williams had told her. He seemed distracted, as if he hoped not paying strict attention to them would make them go away.

After Williams identified himself and Cynthia, Arnold said, "Uh, is there a problem?"

"We just need a brief word with you, sir."

Arnold focused on them reluctantly. He was a plump, tallish man, dressed in a clubby pullover and creased gray slacks. The neatness of his clothing, however, was offset by his thinning brown hair, which curled upward in a kind of mad-scientist nimbus. His eyes blinked rapidly, like the button light on a computer registering some internal activity.

"All right," he said, moving aside for them.

Immediately to the left of the hallway was a room occupied by a man and a young woman, presumably the guests. They were sitting in some wing chairs pulled around a coffee table.

"Hello," Cynthia said.

The young woman, or girl—she seemed not much older than seventeen or eighteen—gave them a sweetly ravishing smile. Her arms and neck were so slender her swollen belly seemed an anomaly, and despite her plain green dress and lack of make-up, she was exquisitely beautiful: long blond hair, gray-green eyes, delicate features. She reminded Cynthia of Botticelli's Flora in *Allegory of Spring*.

Forced to stop, Arnold said, "This is Pastor Brown and his... and Rachel."

Cynthia stepped into the room. Unlike the house's exterior, its elegance was undiminished. No dust and cobwebs. There were built-in white bookcases stocked with decorative sets of books, a Persian rug that covered most of the hardwood floor, an elaborately carved wooden fireplace, and a big painting over the mantel of a handsome, middle-aged woman in fox-hunting garb astride a horse—the icy mother, she supposed.

"Cynthia Westbrook, sheriff's investigator," she said to the pair.

Brown, who'd acknowledged her hello with a stare, now nodded in response. He was a smallish man with short auburn hair. If his dark slacks and white dress shirt were any indication, he didn't readily put aside his ministerial role. His face was what she thought of as Southern rural: knobby-cheeked, thin-lipped, and small eyed, more a bulwark against the world than a receptive surface. In his lap lay an open Bible.

Arnold said, "I'm sorry, Pastor. I don't know what this is about."

"It's all right, Brother Henry," Brown said. "We'll continue when you're finished."

Williams, in a confidential tone, said to Arnold, "It might be best if we talked in private."

"Uh, sure." Arnold glanced uneasily at the girl. "We'll just… this way."

Clever of Williams, she thought, to separate Arnold from the others by insinuating an awkward revelation. He was betting, as she would, that the John sting hadn't acted as a deterrence.

They disappeared down the hall, leaving Cynthia as planned with the guests.

She gestured at the empty chair. "May I?"

"Make yourself at home," Brown said. His delivery of this folksy expression had a kind of impersonal, public quality, as if he were speaking to a crowd.

When she was seated, he said, "We were having our daily Bible reading."

"Sorry to interrupt."

"Our reading was the parable of the lost sheep, as recorded in Matthew. Are you familiar with it?"

"Shepherd leaves the ninety-nine to find the one that's lost."

He nodded approvingly. "Very good. Are you saved, Cynthia?"

Ignoring the question, and its attendant presumption and condescension, she said, "So what brings you to these parts?"

"We are witnessing at all the state's butcheries."

"The women's clinics."

"So called, yes," he said.

"Was it at the women's clinic here you met Mr. Arnold?"

Brown placed a hand on his Bible. "*All things work together for good, to those who love God,*" he intoned. "Our car broke down and Brother Henry saw us walking on the roadside and gave us a ride. Then the Lord moved him to invite us to stay with him."

A picture was emerging. They were evidently without many

resources and in need of Arnold's largesse. "When do you plan on leaving?" she said.

"We wait upon the Lord's instruction."

"What about Mr. Arnold's wishes?"

"If Brother Henry wants us to leave," he said, "that would certainly be a sign. The old woman who paid him a visit, she sent you, didn't she?"

"She asked us to check on things."

"To see if we are taking advantage of him."

Since he'd cut to the chase, she did too. "That's right. Are you?"

"Not at all, as I'm sure he'll tell the other officer."

"Good to hear." She turned to Rachel, who hadn't spoken a word. "When's your baby due?"

"The end of August," Rachel said. Her first utterance, high-pitched and twangy, didn't match her ethereal appearance, but somehow made it more affecting.

"Mr. Arnold didn't say how the two of you are related."

"Rachel is my spiritual wife," Brown answered for her.

Meaning, Cynthia thought, *he'd gotten her pregnant.* "How old are you, Rachel?" she asked.

"Nineteen, ma'am."

"And when's your birthday?"

"October second."

Cynthia did the math using today's date, May 21, as her reference point. Rachel had been of age when she became pregnant, unless she was lying. But that seemed unlikely. She had an air of utter guilelessness.

"I'll tell you what you'd like to know," Brown said. "It's what I say everywhere we go, to the congregations and the good folks like Brother Henry who help us." He leaned toward the girl and took her hand, gazing at her appreciatively as if she were a valuable possession. "Rachel and her family were members of my flock. When her father died, I went to see them, the mother and the sisters. They were living in a trailer park full of alcoholics and drug addicts. I took pity on the whole family, but especially on Rachel. And so it happened. I fell short of God's grace, and this is my penance—to live hand to mouth so I can minister to the lost sheep, the young women who come to the butcheries, by showing them in Rachel and myself the way to salvation."

It was worse than she'd thought. He didn't just use Rachel as a sort of living signboard; he talked about her in her presence, as he was doing now. It was like something out of *The Scarlet Letter*, Dimmesdale on the scaffold with Hester.

Cynthia looked at Rachel, who smiled sweetly at her again. If Brown's road show troubled her, she didn't show it. Indeed, she didn't show anything except a kind of becalmed compliance. "Are you seeing a doctor?" she asked.

"We trust in the Lord," Brown said.

"Well, I doubt the Lord would object to a doctor."

"I could drive her," Arnold said behind her. She looked over her shoulder and saw him and Williams standing in the entrance.

"Good," she said. "I hope you do."

"Thanks for your time, Mr. Arnold," Williams said. And to Brown and Rachel: "You folks have a nice day."

Taking this as her cue, Cynthia joined him in the hall.

At the door Arnold said brightly to Williams, "You ever want to try out the Kalahsnikov, just let me know."

"Will do," Williams said.

When they got in the car, she said, "What was that about a Kalahsnikov?"

"Once he realized I wasn't going to arrest him for consorting with prostitutes, he asked if I'd like to see his gun collection. I said yes, thinking it'd be a chance to observe him. He's got a whole room full of guns, in cabinets and display cases. Some go back to the Revolutionary War, but there's a lot of more recent military stuff. Tommy Guns, Berettas, M-16s, you name it. He said his father started the collection, and he keeps adding to it. It's a pretty big investment, I bet. Maybe that's why his place is going to the dogs. The guns that are functional, he likes to take for a spin at the local shooting range."

"How about his relationship with his guests?"

"If you don't mind," he said, "I'd like to hear your impression of them first."

"Sure. Brown's very controlling." She told him the minister's story about getting Rachel pregnant and then using her to atone for his sin. "Also, it looks like the nosey neighbor's right he persuaded Arnold to protest with them. But persuasion isn't coercion. I don't see they're abusing Arnold, although Brown could be guilty of statutory rape, depending on when he first had sex with Rachel. You could look into that—if you know their full names and where they're from, which I didn't get. Seems like Brown may have controlled me a little too."

"I only asked for Brown's first name, which is George," Williams said. "Guess that makes me guilty of sexism again. According to Arnold they come from the Middle Peninsula, though he didn't know the exact place. But it should be enough to track down Brown. So why do you think he's doing this—his church kick him out because of the girl?"

"Something along those lines. I wonder, too, if he has a wife. The fact he hasn't married Rachel could suggest it."

"Yeah, makes sense. And with all of that, he's still preaching."

"It's what he knows."

"Could be he also believes it."

Williams was not so much defending Brown, she took it, as defending the faith. "In his case," she said, "believing might be less important than acting as if he does. They might amount to the same thing for him. But where do you come out on Arnold? You see any undue influence?"

He shook his head. "No, not undue. But if you ask me, it isn't Brown who's influencing Arnold. It's the girl. He kept mentioning her—said she tidied things up and did the laundry and fixed the meals, even though he didn't want her to, in her condition. I think he's smitten."

"Smitten?"

"What's wrong with that?"

She laughed. "Nothing, except it's sort of old fashioned."

"Well, I guess I'm an old-fashioned guy."

And so he was, she thought. In a good way. His competence had been obvious in their earlier professional contacts, but since then he'd acquired a new seriousness. And though she'd slept with him, and still found him attractive, her basic reaction was approvingly maternal. He was becoming a good man.

Chapter 4

THAT EVENING OVER DINNER SHE told Jack about Arnold and his guests. He listened intently, not interrupting, and when she finished, he said, "Rachel's passivity could be a sign of sexual abuse—not by the minister, necessarily. You say Brown stepped in when her father died? Just speculating, but her father may have abused her, and Brown, even if unwittingly, took over that role."

"I don't know how unwitting it would have been. As I said, he's a controller."

Jack nodded. "One other thing. By putting her on display, he may be punishing her subconsciously for tempting him."

"Even worse. What do you make of Arnold?"

"Your friend said he kept mentioning Rachel."

The word *friend* brought her up. Did Jack suspect anything about her past relations with Steve Williams? If so, it didn't show in his face. "Right," she said.

"And there's Brown's story about Arnold picking them up. He might have done it to be a Good Samaritan, but my guess is he stopped for Rachel. Is she really so pretty?"

"She is."

"And visibly pregnant."

"Very much so."

"To Arnold she might seem the antithesis of the prostitutes he's been with."

"Even though she's pregnant and unwed."

"Like the Virgin Mary. I wonder if he's Catholic. Not that he would have to be to respond to the iconography. Your police friend—"

"Steve Williams," she interrupted.

"He said the mother was cold and aloof, at least in his encounter with her."

She thought of the equestrian painting, the rider's formal smile and dark, remote gaze, and a line from Shelly's "Ozymandias" came to her: *The hand that mocked.* "Maybe she was like that generally," she said. "There was a portrait of her—or so I assume—that chimed with his impression."

"Then it's possible Arnold sees Rachel not just as an ideal of feminine purity, but as a comforting mother figure."

"She's also doing his laundry and making his meals," Cynthia said.

"Well, that would help too," Jack said with a wry smile. "As would her passivity, her blankness. It allows him to read into her whatever he wants."

"So he and Brown both see her in the light of their needs," she said. "*Don't* see her, in other words."

"Unfortunately," Jack said.

His insights sharpened her desire to free Rachel from the two men, especially Brown. Almost anything would be better, she thought, than being the preacher's sexual plaything and traveling exhibit. In her spare time she tried to learn more about him as a means of learning about Rachel. His driver's license showed his place of residence as White Marsh, a little town on the Middle Peninsula about ten miles north of the York River. There were a number of churches in and around White Marsh, four of them Baptist, one Anglican, and one Episcopalian. Disregarding the latter two, she called the Baptist churches. None of them claimed him or knew him, but the secretary at one said he could be the minister fired for "hanky panky" by a little church several miles outside of town. The name of it, she said, was Yahweh something. But that was as far as Cynthia could get. Yahweh Something apparently lacked a telephone number and a website.

She wondered what Steve Williams had found out, but she didn't want to press him; it was his bailiwick and his concern. And then he called her. Having more or less duplicated her method of inquiry, he'd gone a step further. "Shannon and I took the day off," he said, "and drove down to White Marsh."

"Long day," she said.

"Well, I threw in dinner in Williamsburg. Owed her that much for dragging her around White Marsh trying to find somebody who knew something. We finally got lucky at a beauty parlor. Lady having her hair done was a member of Brown's former church and told us the whole story. Not long after he arrived, twelve years ago, he married one of his flock, an eighteen-year-old."

"Sounds familiar."

"Yeah. She gave birth seven months after the wedding. It was a scandal, but the congregation forgave him. So things went along okay until he got Rachel pregnant and Rachel's mom spilled the beans. When his wife heard about it, she kicked him out. I guess she'd evolved since her teenage years—lady said she ran her own nail shop. Anyway, the church kicked him out too, and also Rachel and her family, for good measure. He hung around for a while, living with them in the trailer park and working at a shoe store. But then the two of them took off for parts unknown, as far as the lady knows."

"Got his instructions from the Lord."

"Or didn't want to pay child support—he has three kids."

"No longer giving him the benefit of the doubt?"

"He doesn't deserve it. Rachel's last name, by the way, is Dudley. Possible she was underage when they first had sex, but it wouldn't be easy to prove."

"No," Cynthia said.

"Change of subject. Shannon's decided on the wedding date: August eleven. Give me your address and the shrink's name and we'll send you an invite."

She supplied the information.

"This mean you're coming?" he said.

"With bells on."

Meanwhile, the cases she and Jeff were working did nothing to shake her feeling that the world was spinning out of control. They investigated a double shooting at Gilley's, a rustic roadhouse on 734 below Parkerville. Two men had gotten into an argument, pulled guns from their open-carry holsters, and shot each other. One of them was in the hospital being treated for a thigh wound; the other had run out of Gilley's bleeding from a grazed temple, and was still running. Miraculously, the only collateral damage was to an ancient payphone on the wall.

Jeff, checking his notes, asked Gilley if he had any idea where Earl Latham might have gone.

"His family would know better than me," said Gilley, a cadaverous man with thick eyebrows and a perpetually down-turned mouth.

"To my great surprise," Jeff said, "they don't. In fact, they hardly seem to remember him."

"Well, he talked a lot about hunting. Maybe there's some lodge or something he uses."

"What started the fight?" Jeff said.

"Pickled egg," Gilley said.

"Come again?"

"It was the last one in the bowl, and Marvin, the other guy, fished it out while Earl was reaching for it."

"So did Earl draw his weapon first?"

"Yeah, but Marvin distracted him with the egg. Threw it in his face. Then he pulled his gun too."

"Earl and Marvin know each other?" Jeff said.

"Been coming, both of 'em, for years now."

"So what was the real reason for their… disagreement? One of them boffing the other's wife?"

Gilley frowned. "Naw, I think it was just the egg. And too much beer."

Jeff pointed to the payphone, which had a hole in its black casing below the dial. "The bullet that did that," he said, "you think it might've ricocheted off Earl's head?"

The corners of Gilley's mouth tugged ever so faintly upward, before gravity pulled them down again.

When they stepped outside, Jeff said to her, "Is it just me, or do things seem more out of whack than usual?"

"It's me, too," Cynthia said.

"Something in the water?"

"Something in the air, anyway."

As she drove, Jeff called home to check on Angela, who had the sniffles. Listening to his end of the conversation, she still couldn't quite reconcile this doting father with her wise-ass partner. Sometimes she felt as if she were working with a split personality. His wise-assery had made him persona non grata to Roger, now the division commander, and therefore the last person he should tick off, particularly since he was the only black detective in Crimes Against Persons. Racism, unconscious or otherwise, lurked just beneath the surface here as it did in every organization. No one would admit to it, of course, but it was as evident to her as the sexism she had to deal with—the dirty jokes told in her hearing, the "mansplaining," the speaking over her at meetings. Her parallel experience was probably one of the reasons she and Jeff had hit it off from the beginning.

Jeff, however, didn't seem to regard either his attitude or his color as a drawback. He assumed he had a bright future in the department, and maybe he was right. His ability had made him the youngest person, black or white, ever promoted to the unit; and he was also very photogenic, not as important an asset, perhaps, as a willingness to suck up, but not negligible either. His only shortcoming, physically speaking, was his stature; he was a good six or seven inches shorter than her 6'2". But in a way this created another bond between them: neither conformed to the standard height-range for their genders. Early on, Rick Draper had joked to Jeff in her presence, managing to insult them both, "You know, you oughta get some elevator shoes, so the two of you match up better."

"Like you and Ennis," Jeff said.

Draper eyed him uneasily. "Yeah."

"That Ennis is a smart guy."

"So?" Draper said.

"I'm just saying, if we're talking about matching up."

"You calling me dumb?"

"Everything's relative, isn't it?" Jeff said. "Height, intelligence, social skills."

Draper, unable to compete, stormed off.

The day they arrested Earl Latham, he of the hard skull, in a hunting cabin near the Maryland border, she got home late. She showered and changed into her robe while Jack re-heated her dinner, and after she'd eaten it, they read for a while on the couch. Then they went to bed, where, lights out, he gave her a long kiss.

"I know you're tired," he said. "I'm not necessarily trying to start anything."

"Well, that's good, since I'm a woman past her prime."

Before he could object, she kissed him back, and one thing led to another, and another.

Afterward, as she lay in the dark listening to his slow, deep breathing, she thought of Steve and Shannon, and Jeff and his wife Denise. Jack had married young like them and ended up divorced, and she'd gone through a number of brief affairs, calling it quits before any of them could get serious. She and Jack were each other's chance at something solid and long-lasting. But she was thirty-five and he was forty-six, and their love, tinged with experience and regret, could never be the shiny thing young love was. Did that make it less? No, she decided. Any couple would be lucky to have what they had. She thought of unlucky Rachel, and a vision of the girl's beautiful, becalmed face arose in her mind. Like Sleeping Beauty, Rachel was under a spell. What would it take to awaken her? Cynthia tried to imagine the circumstances, but sleep had cast its own spell on her, and her brain, succumbing, threw up a vision of Rachel with flowers in her hair, like Botticelli's Flora.

The muted dinging of her phone woke her. She fetched it from the night table and glanced at the time: 12:03. Next to her, Jack stirred. Answering silently, she got out of bed and went down the hall. Now that she and Jeff, the identified caller, were both sharing their beds with someone, they'd worked out a system for late-night communications: the initiator remained silent until the other had spoken.

"Okay," she said when she reached the den.

"You didn't see the late-night news, did you?" he said.

Something in his voice made her pulse leap. "No."

"The women's clinic in North Hill was bombed, and there are some deaths, one of them a cop. I called the North Hill station and they put Roger on. He passed me off to Ennis—obviously, we weren't invited—and I badgered some details out of Ennis. Bomb went off around ten. Arson squad says it was dynamite, a lot of dynamite, placed behind a dumpster and set off by a timer.

The clinic was closed for the day, but there were at least two bodies inside, not identified yet—though one's probably the doctor whose car they found around back. They also found a body outside, the cop. They figure he spotted the tail-end of the doctor's car, just a few inches showing, Ennis thinks—so he must've been super attentive. He drove back to take a look, and he was standing near the building when the bomb went off."

Jeff stopped, but she didn't disturb the silence by asking who it was.

"Word is," Jeff said, "it's Steve Williams."

Chapter 5

SHE DIDN'T KNOW WHAT TO do. As Jeff said, they hadn't been invited. But she couldn't go back to sleep. She dressed in the set of clothes she'd begun keeping in the coat closet, got her wallet, keys, and badge from the hall bureau, and stuck a note on the fridge that said simply "Clinic bombed," relying on the news to tell Jack the rest. Then she slipped quietly out the door.

She drove south to Calvary and northwest on 734, going past Gilley's and the rows of John Deere tractors and the saddlery with the life-sized statue of a white horse on the roof, her headlights plowing through the darkness but leaving no furrow, the night inky black in the rear-view mirror. Her thoughts about young love came back to her, and she realized she'd neglected to factor in the uncertainty of everything. No stage of life was sacrosanct. Steve Williams and Shannon had known a few weeks or months of happiness together, and that was the end of it.

A number of vehicles were parked in front of the smallish cinderblock North Hill station, and a few reporters and a couple of camera operators stood on the sidewalk awaiting updates. She parked a block up, walked back, and showed her badge to the cop at the main desk, who nodded her through to the big central room. Huddled near the back, not far from Steve Williams' empty desk, were Sheriff Sampson, the North Hill police chief, Roger, Draper, and Ennis. Sampson was doing the talking. In a tailored uniform that flattered his gym-enhanced physique, he was ready for his close-up even at one a.m. Roger, who looked as though he'd never been near a tailor or a gym, spotted her first, and Sampson, noticing his surprised expression, followed his gaze and held up a hand to her like a traffic cop. She stopped. Sampson said something to Roger, who began walking toward her, eyes averted.

As always she braced herself a little for Roger. Though he was never less than professional with her, there was a subtext. He tended to show up at the coffee table when she did, and to pass by her desk instead of taking the more direct routes between his office and everywhere else. Also, his largely silent attentions had escalated since his divorce. More than happenstance would allow, he arrived at the building entrance when she did and rode the elevator up with her. Jeff, taking note, teased him subtly but mercilessly. "You need to start dating," he'd advise Roger with apparent sincerity. "Best thing for you. Have you checked out that girl in Evidence—the tall one?"

"Hi, Cynthia," Roger said with a glassy-eyed stare. "Sorry, but the sheriff wants you to leave, since you aren't part of the investigation."

"Was it Steve Williams?" she said.

"Yeah. You know him?"

"I helped him with something not long ago."

A voice said, "Talking to them pro-lifers, right?"

They both turned toward the speaker, a fat, gray-haired cop at a desk.

"What pro-lifers?" Roger said.

"Couple from out of town been protesting at the clinic. They're staying with a local guy Steve asked me about."

"You know their names?" Roger asked her, transparently eager to have something to show Sampson.

"I doubt they had anything to do with this," she said.

"Still, we'll need to check them out." He fetched a notebook from his coat pocket, bringing up with it a wad of tissue that landed on the cop's desk. "Sorry," he said, and stuffed the tissue back in his pocket. He looked at her expectantly, and she gave him the names.

"Maybe the sheriff will bring you in," he said, "once I show him this."

She wasn't counting on it. When Sampson was division commander, he'd been jealous of the attention she received for the serial-murder case, even though she'd refused interviews and hidden out for a time at Sally's. Since then all the higher-profile cases had gone to other investigators. Roger, his successor and beneficiary, was evidently under orders to keep her and Jeff out of the spotlight, an injustice Jeff was inclined to point out to him. "So whataya got for us today?" he'd say to Roger. "Trespassing? Expectorating in public? Tooth fairy didn't pay up?" Ironically, her success might have helped Sampson in his bid for sheriff, but it might also be the deepest source of his dislike: he didn't want to owe her.

"I better get back," Roger said, his expression moony again. "Maybe you should…"

"Yeah, I'm leaving. Good luck with the case."

The old cop, watching Roger go, said, "He your boss?"

"Yep."

"My sympathies. You know Steve well?"

"Not too well, no."

"He was getting married."

"I did know that," she said.

"Damn shame," the old cop said. "He was a good man."

On her way out she noticed a young woman in a campus-security uniform at the front desk. *Shannon,* she thought immediately. Pretty profile, short dark hair, eye-catching figure despite the unflattering uniform. She stopped and listened.

"But if it wasn't him," the woman was saying, "couldn't you at least tell me that?"

"Sorry, ma'am," the desk cop said, "we can't release any information until the family's been contacted."

"But I'm—" She stopped herself. "So it was him, that's what you're saying, isn't it?"

The cop shook his head. "I'm sorry. It's not up to me."

Cynthia went over to her. "Shannon," she said, drawing her attention. "I'm Cynthia Westbrook—sheriff's department."

"I know who you are. I saw you on TV."

"Why don't we go outside and talk?"

Shannon's face registered the meaning of this. "Okay," she said.

Cynthia led her to the car and opened the back door. "More private in here," she said. She went around to the other side and got in and faced Shannon.

"I'm sorry," she said. "It was Steve."

Shannon's eyes, faintly luminescent in the ambient street light, seemed to stare inward at the hard truth. When they focused again on Cynthia, she said, "Why was he there?"

"He was doing his job. He spotted a car behind the clinic and went back to investigate. That's when the bomb went off."

"Was he… did he suffer?"

"I don't know. My guess is no. It was probably instantaneous."

"I hope so," Shannon said. Then she slumped forward and began a high-pitched keening. In the cramped backseat of the Corolla, all Cynthia could do was grip the girl's hands and let her mourn, for however long it took. But after a few seconds, the keening abruptly ceased, and Shannon, freeing her hands, wiped at her face.

"It's all right," Cynthia said. "You don't have to hold it in for my sake."

"No, I need to tell his family. They've been trying to reach him, too, ever since the news report. Can I tell them?"

The names of the victims, or the known ones anyway, would be announced soon enough, but word could still get back to Sampson that someone had leaked the information. So be it. "Sure," she said. "What about your family? Do they live around here?"

"Front Royal," Shannon said.

"You should tell them, too."

"I will."

They sat for a while longer in silence.

"I didn't just see you on TV," Shannon said. "Steve talked about you. He really admired you."

Cynthia looked for some sign Steve had said more than that, though it wasn't the kind of thing men tell their fiancées, and as far as she knew, he'd never told anyone else, either. "I felt the same way about him," she said. "He was a good cop."

"Yes, he was," Shannon said.

The *was* seemed to hang in the air between them.

"I better go," Shannon said. "Thank you."

She climbed out of the car and headed toward the station. Cynthia watched her through the rear window. Her gait was a little unsteady, as if she'd received a blow but withstood it. Steve had called her *feisty*, and he was right. She'd need to be. She'd have to let go of the future she'd imagined for herself, and turn her thoughts from a wedding to a funeral. Emily Dickinson had said it best, as usual: *The sweeping up the heart, and putting love away.*

Leaving town, Cynthia went a few blocks out of her way and drove slowly past the clinic. An arson-squad van and some sheriff cars were parked in front of it, partly blocking the view, but she could see enough to know the devastation was total. Beyond the yellow police tape and a narrow, upright piece of the facade, with the letters *WOM* near its top, balloon lights cast a brilliant white glow over heaps of splintered boards and drywall fragments and overturned furniture and twisted pipes and wires sprouting like weeds. Investigators in padded vests and visored helmets were searching through the rubble, looking for clues or perhaps other victims. The structures on either side, a bike shop and a small office building with a For Rent sign out front, had been damaged too, their adjacent walls blown away, revealing a tangle of bikes in one and empty, cave-like spaces in the other. The bomb seemingly had been set to go off when nobody was around. But if that was the case, the bomber hadn't counted on an after-hours use of the clinic, or on Steve Williams showing up at just the wrong moment.

In the grip of strong emotion, of several emotions—grief, yes, and sadness for Shannon and the Williams family, and frustration at being kept out of the investigation, and regret she couldn't be completely candid with Jack about Steve—she pulled over on the curb and sat with the engine running. The memory of her post-sex conversation with Steve floated into her mind. Once he'd realized playtime was over, he'd asked about her family, and though she'd told him no more than she had anyone else, his delicate probing had impressed her as sincere. That was partly why, when she was leaving, she'd blurted out her mother's murder to him, and so confronted the trauma that Jack, without knowing its nature, had guessed was the cause of her insomnia. Until then she'd existed in a sort of a trance, like Rachel Dudley.

She remembered something else. When Steve was driving them back from Arnold's, she'd observed to herself that he was becoming a good man. It was a mistaken, condescending appraisal. He was already a good man, as the old cop had said, and he would've been a good husband, and a good father. If the world weren't spinning out of control.

Chapter 6

WHEN SHE GOT HOME, SHE didn't feel like going back to sleep, so she read yesterday's Post as a distraction, though it was hardly that. Shootings here and there. The Syrian government destroying a village and killing dozens of children. The Potomac declared the most endangered river in America, which was somehow apt. But at last she reached the desired stage where her brain could no longer process a sentence, and the next thing she knew she was waking up to sunlit curtains and muted kitchen noises.

Jack was fixing pancakes. Seeing her in the kitchen doorway, he said, "Thought you could use something substantial."

His method was to put the cakes in the oven until he'd cooked them all, and then serve them. Once he'd slipped a stack onto each plate, he said, "I heard the news on the radio, but they didn't identify the police officer."

"Steve Williams," she said.

"The one you saw the abortion protesters with?"

She nodded.

"You didn't say so, but I got the impression you'd worked with him before."

"Couple of times, yes."

"Then it must have been quite a blow."

"Always is when it's a fellow cop. I saw his fiancée at the police station. They weren't telling her anything, so I did."

Jack placed his hand on hers. "Hard night," he said.

Whether he meant more than this wasn't clear.

She showered and dressed and went in to work. Jeff was already there, writing up the report on the pickled-egg shooting. She told him about her visit to the North Hill station.

"Well, I've got one bit of good news," he said. "Grapevine has it the FBI's taking over the case. So Sampson will be demoted to water boy."

At noon she went down to see Charles, the medical examiner, anticipating she'd find him in his office at lunch time. Food was his avocation—he wrote occasional restaurant reviews for the local paper—and her intention was to avoid talking to him in his shining kingdom of death. As essential as autopsies were, they'd always felt to her like a violation of the dead: the torso sliced open and the ribs cut away, the glistening organs removed, the grooved brain scooped from the skull. More importantly, Charles might be working on Steve, and that would be a memory she didn't want to have.

She knocked on his door.

"Enter!" he called.

A rotund man with a cherub's cheeks and bee-stung lips, he smiled up at her from behind his desk, on which sat several Styrofoam containers. "Ah, Cynthia," he said. "I was just about to have my lunch. A repast from the new Indian restaurant down the street." He waved a chubby hand over the boxes. "Chicken Tikka Masala, Lamb Vindallu, and Mango Walla with shrimp. Care to partake?"

"Thanks, but no thanks, Charles. I was wondering if you were doing the autopsies on the bombing victims."

"Of course. When it's one of our own, everything revolves around that. I haven't slept since I visited the crime scene."

"Sorry."

He shrugged. "Not a complaint, merely a statement of fact."

"The officer, Steve Williams—you know the specific cause of death?"

"Crushed, basically. The explosion flipped a metal dumpster on him. But at least, for his family's sake, he's in one piece. Without the dumpster there, he would have been ripped apart."

Or he might have seen the bomb, she thought, *and disarmed it or tossed it away.*

"Sure you won't have any?" said Charles, opening a box. A spicy aroma wafted her way.

"Yes. One other thing—who's the woman?"

"Still Ms. Doe to me. But why would you need to ask?"

"Not my case."

"Ah."

She thanked him and went back up. Jeff informed her they'd been assigned a dog-napping. "At least it isn't a hamster," he said. "We can still hold our heads high."

They drove to the neighborhood where the dog had been snatched and spoke to the distraught owners, a middle-aged couple, in their home. On the lamp table next to them was a picture of the dog, a Corgi, marching in the Corgi contingent of the Parkerville Christmas parade.

Looking at Cynthia, the husband said, "We were taking our evening walk, and this black man came from the other direction. He wasn't anyone I'd seen before. You don't usually see..."

"Oh, no," the wife said. "Never. But he said how cute Luna was, and he knelt and petted her."

"Then a van stopped," the husband said, "and he grabbed her and jumped in, and they sped off."

"Why would anybody do that?" the wife said.

"To sell her," Jeff said, not elaborating. The customer could be a medical lab or a dogfighter in need of "bait" for training purposes. "Can you describe the guy?"

"He was sort of skinny," the wife said.

"But strong," added the husband, perhaps to justify not having fought for his dog. "He jerked the leash right out of my hand. And like we said, he was black." This last adjective he directed specifically to Cynthia, not so much out of embarrassment, it seemed to her, as in racial solidarity, one white person to another.

"The dog's name is Luna?" Jeff said. "Like *lunatic* without the *tic*?"

"That's right," the husband said, frowning.

"Just need to get the spelling right," Jeff said.

They questioned them for a few more minutes, learning the kidnapper's t-shirt was green or yellow, the van was white or yellow, and the driver was a black man or a black woman. Then they interviewed a few of his neighbors on the chance they'd seen something, but nobody had.

"Only one thing left to do," Jeff said to her. "Turn myself in for being black."

"A noble gesture, but it won't solve the crime."

"Maybe if I think hard enough, I'll remember what I did with the dog."

At headquarters, they checked the files for other dog-nappings in the area, and while they were doing this, someone turned on the TV. A news conference was underway outside the North Hill station. Sampson, at the microphone, presented the basic facts for public consumption and named the victims: Officer Steven Williams; Dr. Peter Beatty, long associated with the clinic; and Kristen Gates, age nineteen.

The reporters went silent for a moment, and then one of them asked the obvious question: "Is that General Gates's daughter?"

"Yes," Sampson said, and turned the microphone over to the FBI agent heading the investigation.

"Holy mackerel," Jeff said. "Was the General's daughter having a secret abortion?"

"Be my guess," she said.

"This will sink him."

"Assuming he wants to stay in the water."

That night at home, she and Jack watched the local evening news. Nothing new from Sampson or the FBI, but there was video of another press conference held later in the day, this one called by Gates's campaign manager. The General had moved to North Hill after a stint at the Pentagon, so the campaign manager, a young blond woman, was standing outside his headquarters around the corner from the North Hill police station. "I have a statement from General Gates," she said. "After I read it, I won't be taking any questions." She paused, staring at the paper in her hands, seemingly trying to collect herself: "Betty and I," she began, "are still coming to grips with the loss of our precious daughter. We ask for time to grieve in private. We do not know why Kristen was at the North Hill Clinic for Women. But that matters far less to us than the fact her life has been cut short. We take comfort in our faith that she's now with God, safe from all harm."

There were questions, of course, shouted rapid fire at the young woman. But she only said, "The General will address you himself at a later time," and turned and entered the building.

"Poor man," said Jack, whose daughter was around the age of Kristen Gates.

Chapter 7

"TOUNE LEFT IN THREE-HUNDRED YARDS," Bugs Bunny said, and when she did, waving at a deputy beside his car, there was a burst of the Looney Tunes theme and Bugs telling her, "Congrats! You've arrived at your destah-*nation*!"

Bugs was the new navigation app on Jeff's phone. She suspected he'd chosen it to annoy her, which was why she hadn't said anything about it. She followed the dirt road another thirty yards through dense woods and around a curve to a dead end occupied by a dirty black Mustang. Another sheriff's car was parked a few feet short of it, and the deputy standing next to it looked to be about fifteen.

Adopting a stern tone, conducive in her experience to honesty, she said, "You touch anything?"

"No, ma'am," the deputy said.

This was one drawback to a stern tone. She didn't know what she disliked more, being ogled or being called ma'am.

"Did you run the plates?" she said less severely.

He handed her his phone. The screen showed a driver's license issued to a Jason Bell, age twenty-nine by her calculation, of

Dumfries, Virginia. Dumfries was a little town about seventy miles southeast of North Hill, which raised the question of what Bell was doing up here.

She gave him back the phone, along with her card. "Send it to me," she said.

"Yes'um."

"I understand somebody alerted you."

"Old boy lives out this way. He was hunting."

"I didn't know this was hunting season."

"Spring turkey. Well, technically that ended a couple days ago, but I let it go, considering."

Considering the dead man in the Mustang, he meant. She nodded.

"I asked him," the deputy said, "if he'd come by this way earlier. He said yesterday morning, and the car wasn't here."

"Oh. Good work."

Jeff, humming to himself, an unnatural death being of greater interest to him than a dog-napping, had moved some distance away and was taking pictures with his phone. She went over to the car and looked in through the rolled-down driver's window. Jason Bell, in black t-shirt and jeans, radiated the unsettling stillness of the dead. He had a high forehead and a strong nose. His brown hair was close cut, his jaw stubbled, his gray eyes open and empty. He was slumped away from her as if to display the ragged red hole in his temple, where several flies were feeding.

Waving the flies away, she examined the hole. The charring as well as the stellate pattern indicated contact with a gun muzzle. She placed her gloved hand on his shoulder. He was still in rigor, which accorded with the timeline of the hunter's story. She leaned in and saw a gun, a Glock, lying beside his left foot. Keys in the ignition. On the passenger seat, an empty liquor bottle. What appeared to be a slug was lodged in the plastic fitting of the passenger door. If that's what it was, the bullet's path would have been downward, the typical trajectory in a suicide headshot, but usually not quite so steep as this one.

She said to Jeff, now aiming his phone through the windshield, "Can you see an exit wound?"

"Lemme try the passenger window."

Since it was also open, he leaned in. "Hard to tell, because of the way his head is," he said, "but there's some blood and stuff level with his cheek bone."

"That would fit with where the slug might be."

She pointed to the spot in the door, and he looked down and said, "Oh, yeah." He held the phone inside, snapped a picture, and checked the image. Then he took some shots of the body. When he was done, he went around behind the car.

"Tire tracks back here," he said.

Cynthia turned to the boyish deputy. "Did you drive up over there?"

"No, ma'am."

Jeff photographed the tracks and joined her near the body, getting more pictures of the corpse from this side, and of the gun on the floor.

"What do you think?" she said.

"Left-hander. Entry wound's in the left temple, the gun's where it is."

"Even if you're a lefty, it'd be a little awkward to do it on the door side. There's less room to raise your arm. Easier to use the other hand."

"He could've stuck his arm out the window."

"True," she said. "Which would explain the path of the bullet. Lifting his elbow might have caused him to point the gun down at that angle. But what about the tire tracks?"

"Hasn't rained in a few days, has it?" Jeff said.

"No." She looked around. No puddles on the ground, the

surrounding trees dry. For a moment, her attention wandered to the beauty of the woods, so out of keeping with the human scene. The tender new foliage stirred in a morning breeze, and the forest depths had a soft green glow, shot through here and there with rays of unfiltered light. Not that the forest wasn't also a place of death. If you looked hard enough, you'd find the picked-over corpses of birds and other animals. But at least those deaths helped to perpetuate a natural order; they weren't pointless like Jason Bell's, however it had happened.

"So the tracks could predate our guy," Jeff said. "This is a good make-out place."

"Let's get a tech out here anyway to do an impression and dust for prints."

"We should get the hunter's prints too," Jeff said, "in case he touched anything."

"Right. And I'll ask Charles to check the blood alcohol, before the body is much further along."

❉ ❉ ❉

They returned to the station in the early afternoon, having pissed off Larry, the tech, who thought they were wasting his time with an obvious suicide. The hunter they'd taken care of themselves, to avoid Larry's wrath. While Jeff was downstairs looking at personal effects, she searched for Bell in the system. There was a handgun registered to him—she'd need to compare serial numbers—and a DUI from 2010, license suspended for a year. Otherwise, nothing. She did a White Pages search for other Bells in Dumfries, found only one, an Alice Bell, and called the number. A woman answered.

Having identified herself, Cynthia said, "Is this Ms. Bell?"

"No, but she can't talk on the phone. She had a stroke."

"Are you her helper?"

"I'm her daughter, Amber Warren."

"Do you know a Jason Bell, Ms. Warren?"

"He's my brother."

Being the bearer of bad news was never easy, and it was the second time she'd done it in as many days. "I'm sorry to tell you," she said, "but he died of a gunshot wound, apparently self-inflicted. His body was discovered this morning in his car, outside of North Hill."

Silence. She let it sink in.

"You're saying he killed himself," Alice Warren said.

"It looks that way."

Another long pause, and then: "What do I do?"

"We'll need a relative to identify the body, here at the sheriff's office in Parkerville. It doesn't have to be you."

"I'll come. There isn't anybody else."

"Do you know what he was doing in North Hill?"

"He'd heard General Gates was holding a town-hall meeting up there, and he wanted to tell him about his problems with the VA."

"When was the town hall?"

"Two weeks ago. He called the day after he got there and said he might be working for the campaign. I guess they took him on, but I don't know." Amber Warren's voice had developed a quaver. "It was the last I heard from him. I should've called him, but I didn't."

"All right, Ms. Warren. Thank you."

"I'll be there in the morning if I can change my shift and arrange things with the sitter."

"Take your time," Cynthia said, and gave her the cell number.

Hanging up, she thought it a little odd that Jason Bell had a connection to Gates, and both Bell and Gates's daughter were now dead. Odd but probably just a coincidence. Like Kristen Gates being in the North Hill women's clinic, or Steve Williams driving by at exactly the wrong moment.

Chapter 8

THE NEXT MORNING SHE AND Jeff were about to leave the station—Jeff had found a scrap of paper in Bell's wallet with the name and address of a motel scrawled on it—when Amber Warren called and said she'd be arriving in a couple of hours. So they sat tight and Cynthia phoned Sandy, the part-time grief counselor, to alert her.

Amber Warren showed up in a dark blue dress suit, as if she were attending a funeral. She was a small woman with her brother's gray eyes and prominent nose. But she looked a good deal older than he; indeed, she could have passed for his mother. After she introduced herself, she fell silent, nodding to Sandy when Cynthia introduced her, and tightening her lips at their expressions of condolence.

Sandy said to her, "We'll be going downstairs because it's more private. We won't view Jason's body directly. I'll show you the picture I have here on my clipboard."

Amber Warren stared at the folder on the clipboard, then looked at Cynthia. "Can you come too?" she said.

Cynthia glanced at Sandy, who said, "Of course she can."

They took the elevator down to Charles's empty office, which smelled faintly of spicy food, and Sandy pulled three chairs together to form a little circle. "What you'll see," she said, "is Jason's face with a blue sheet around it, like they use in an operating room. His eyes are closed. He'll look paler than you remember, and there's a small wound in his left temple, and a larger one below the right temple. Okay? I won't show you the picture until you tell me to."

"I'm ready," Amber Warren whispered.

Sandy pulled the photograph from the folder and held it out. Amber Warren took it from her and studied it. "Yes," she said finally, "that's Jason. That's my brother."

"There's no hurry," Sandy said. "We'll just sit here until you're ready to leave. I have some information about agencies in your area that might be of help, but before I give you that, do you have any questions?"

As if she hadn't heard, Amber Warren said, "He was five when our daddy died. I was thirteen, and Momma had to work, so I took care of him a lot of the time. I guess you could say I was like his second mother." She looked at the picture again. "Daddy's death was harder on him than me, I think, because he was a boy. He didn't have anyone to show him how to be a man. Being tough and strong, that was his idea of a man."

Sandy, taking her lead, said, "I understand he was a veteran."

"He joined the Army right after 9/11," Amber Warren said. "They sent him to Afghanistan and Iraq, and it changed him. He'd always had a sweet side, but when he got out of the Army, he was just angry all the time. And drinking too much. So he couldn't hold a job. I tried to talk him into getting help from the VA, but he wouldn't admit there was anything wrong. Then his girlfriend broke up with him, and he got arrested for drunk driving. So I tried again, and this time he went to the VA and filled out a long form, and they turned him down. Which made him even angrier."

She stopped, her eyes shiny with tears. "I should've done more."

Sandy put her hand on the woman's arm. "From what you've

said, you did everything you could."

Amber Warren shook her head. "When he came back I resented him for not helping with Momma, and being half drunk all the time, like my ex-husband. I didn't try hard enough to understand him. I was no better than the VA. They said he couldn't prove he had a head trauma, but so what? His job was to dispose of bombs. Imagine doing that knowing what could happen to you. And he didn't just know it—he saw a friend get blown up. You can't go through those things without being hurt."

The reference to bombs caught Cynthia's attention. She thought about it as Sandy handed Amber Warren a list of agencies and went over it with her. Here was a second coincidence even more compelling than the first: a man who'd come to see Gates, whose daughter had been killed by an explosion, was himself an explosives expert. But why would Bell have planted the dynamite? And if he'd done it, why would he then have killed himself?

"When can I take him home?" Amber Warren said.

"Cynthia?" said Sandy.

"Soon, Ms. Warren. I'll call you. There's still more… procedure."

As they rode the elevator to the first floor, Cynthia glanced at Amber Warren's haggard, sorrowful face—a record of an unhappy life. Childhood cut short, bad marriage, invalid mother, and now a dead brother she thought she'd failed. Thirty-seven going on sixty. It would be cruel to add to her woe by suggesting a link between Jason and the clinic bombing, yet this was also an opportunity. Trying to tread carefully, she said, "So was your brother interested in politics?"

"No," Amber Warren said. "He wasn't political. Coming up here wasn't political; it was personal. I was surprised when he said he might work for the General, but I hoped it'd be a good thing for him." Her eyes filled again with tears. "And for me too, if he wasn't around."

At the exit, she said, "Thank you" to each of them. Then she moved past the door Cynthia held open for her and disappeared into the mild day.

Chapter 9

CYNTHIA FOUND JEFF AT HIS desk talking, apparently, to Angela, since his voice was in the falsetto range. Seeing her coming, he said, "Daddy's got to go, honey. Bye, Bye." Then in his normal baritone he said goodbye to Denise.

"She talking back yet?" Cynthia said.

"Always. I get no respect."

"Angela."

Jeff grinned. "Coming along. She calls me *Daboo*. Well, it's either me or her stuffed bunny. We might be sort of interchangeable at this point."

Cynthia told him about Jason Bell's difficulties and Army job.

"A bomb expert," he said. "Pretty big coincidence."

"Let's say it's more than that. Care to speculate?"

"Okay. Maybe Bell comes up here to see Gates and blow up the clinic. But when he hears that Gates's daughter, along with the others, was killed in the explosion, he offs himself in remorse."

"So he had two reasons for coming up?"

"Possibly. No law against it," he said.

"But there's a principle. Occam's Razor. The simpler the explanation, the better. Also, his sister told me he wasn't political, and she'd probably know."

"Okay, reset. He meets somebody at the town hall, maybe another vet, and they get to talking, and this other guy, after learning what Bell used to do, offers to pay him to blow up the clinic—and Bell, who's been out of work, agrees."

"I doubt you'd find a rabid anti-abortionist at a Gates town hall. Gates is fairly moderate, for a conservative."

"But if my hypothetical guy's a vet, he could've come for the same reason Bell did, plus being rabid on abortion."

"Two reasons again."

"Maybe Occam shaves a little too closely sometimes. Anyway, it would explain why Bell hung around for a couple of weeks. To plan the bombing."

"He called his sister and told her he might go to work for Gates," Cynthia said. "It's a reason for him to stay that doesn't advance your theory."

"Did he go to work for Gates?"

"I don't know."

"Well, that could've been a lie to account for his staying. We could check it out with the Gates campaign. And if somebody gave him money, we could try to find it."

"Still doesn't feel right," she said. "Coincidence looms too large. Bell happened to meet a Gates supporter willing and able to pay him, and Gates's daughter happened to be at the clinic when it was bombed."

"But a coincidence is what got us started: Bell, a bomb expert, was in town when the bomb went off."

"True enough," she said.

"So what do we do?"

"Follow up on your ideas and see if they take us anywhere."

"That doesn't exactly sound like a ringing endorsement."

"Nope."

Jeff grinned. "On the other hand, you came up with squat."

They checked Bell's personal effects again, looking for anything that might lead to money or a local contact. Nothing. The calls on his phone, none more recent than two weeks, were all to the Dumfries area code. These would have to be checked out, but they didn't look promising.

They next went to the impound lot and did a search of the Mustang, checking the dash compartment and side pockets, the spaces between and under the seats, the trunk and wheel boot and trunk-lid inner cover, the engine area, and the insides of the hubcaps. If necessary, they'd get the techs to do a more thorough job, but at the moment they had other fish to fry.

As she drove them to the motel whose name Bell had written down, the Wayside Inn on the west side of North Hill, Jeff said, "Question. If this turns out to be where he stayed, why didn't he kill himself there?"

"That's crossed my mind too."

"Maybe those tire tracks at the scene *are* relevant. Maybe the terrorist vet met him there, got him drunk, and killed him, making it look like suicide."

"What about your earlier theory that Bell was remorseful?"

"He could've been remorseful, and the terrorist vet played on that to get him drunk."

"Your terrorist vet is turning into some kind of master criminal. Let's shelve him for a while."

The Wayside was a weathered, single-story U-shaped structure whose pot-holed lot was empty except for a pickup with a barbecue grill in the truck bed. She'd last seen it when she was searching for Mike Fallon, who'd stayed here while doing his personal investigation into his niece's disappearance. She parked in front of the manager's office and they went inside.

The desk clerk, a scrawny guy with tats on his forearms and thinning gray hair pulled into a ponytail, made them as cops before they said anything, which didn't speak well of him.

"What can I do for you, officers?" he said, giving them a nicotine-stained smile.

"You got a guest named Jason Bell?" Jeff said.

"That rings a bell," he said, and smiled again. He checked on his computer, an object as battered-looking as he. "Room 117. Paid up through the end of the week. He in some kinda trouble?"

"You could say that," Jeff said. "He's dead."

"Oh. I guess you'd like to see his room, then."

He gave them the key, and they walked down to the room and unlocked the door. Musty smell. Dirty green shag carpet. Twin beds with corded brown spreads, the cords worn off in places. Small dresser with cigarette burns along the edge. TV bolted high on the wall.

"I think I've answered my question," Jeff said. "Who would want to die here?"

Or stay here. But Bell hadn't seemed to do much of that. No books or magazines, no trash, the beds neatly made. The room had a tidy, military air that the four empty liquor bottles didn't detract from. He'd lined them up against the wall. *Dead soldiers,* she thought, remembering the old slang term.

There was no suitcase, which fit the sister's story he'd only come up for the town hall. But one of the dresser drawers held a new-looking pair of jeans, a red t-shirt, and a couple of pairs of boxer shorts; and in the tiny bathroom there were some socks hanging over the shower bar and some toiletries on the sink counter. They checked around as thoroughly as they could, looking under the bed and between the mattress and the box springs, peeling off the felt bottom on the lamp, and removing the plastic grid from the window air conditioner.

"Batting zero," Jeff said.

"Or confirming a suicide unrelated to the bombing."

"Pony-tail could have taken the money, or a maid."

"I wouldn't bet on a maid having come in here," she said.

They called tech and went back to the office. Cynthia, returning the key, told the clerk somebody would be coming by to collect Bell's things. "Have you been in his room?" she said.

"No, ma'am. No reason to."

"How about maid service?"

"Shelia, the maid, she cleans when somebody checks out."

"What about fresh towels?"

"They can come to me for that, but we don't encourage it."

"Bell have any visitors you know of?" she said.

The clerk shook his head. "But I don't pay much attention. I try to stay out of the guests' business."

"Your current guest," Jeff said, "the one with the grill in his truck? You might want to get into his business a little. If he does his grilling there, he could blow himself up and burn the whole place down."

"Yes, sir," the clerk said. "I'll certainly see to that."

"Good man," said Jeff, deadpan.

Driving back through North Hill, Cynthia stopped at Gates's headquarters. They could see some people through the storefront window, so they went in. The place had been cleared out. The desktops were empty, the walls bare, the trashcans full. Two college-age boys were stacking boxes in a corner. The other person in the room was the blond campaign manager who'd read Gates's statement to the press.

"Can I help you?" the woman said. In person she looked more attractive than she had on TV. Her pale face, which the camera had flattened and simplified, had interesting planes and nuances, the nose shapely and the bright hazel eyes almond-shaped.

Cynthia introduced herself and Jeff.

"Ashley Hunter," the woman said. "I guess this is about the General's daughter. But I've already told the FBI everything I know, so I doubt I can be of any use."

"Actually," Cynthia said, "it's about something else." She found Bell's driver's license on her phone and showed it. "Recognize this man?"

Ashley Hunter examined the picture. "He does look familiar."

"He attended the town hall meeting in North Hill a couple of weeks ago."

"Oh, yes. That helps. After the meeting, a number of people lined up to talk to the General, and I think he may have been one of them."

"Did Gates give him a job?"

"A job? Not to my knowledge. The General's a kind man, and it's possible he indicated there might be something. But this person would have had to come to me, and he didn't."

"All right, thanks," Cynthia said.

"Surely. If I remember anything else, I'll let you know. Do you have a card?"

Cynthia gave her one.

"As you can see, we're closing up shop. The General's withdrawing from the race."

"Sorry to hear it."

"Yes. He's a man with a lot of integrity, not such a common thing in politics these days. The FBI told him they're going to announce his daughter was pregnant—to prepare him, I guess, for the fallout. But he'd already made up his mind to quit."

Ashley Hunter extended her hand to Cynthia, who shook it. "Good luck with your investigation," she said.

When they were outside, Jeff said, "I think you have an admirer."

"What do you mean?" she asked, although she knew.

"Ashley Hunter. I wouldn't be surprised if she calls you to say she couldn't think of anything."

"And what leads you to this conclusion?"

"My observational skills. She only had eyes for you."

"I see. Your vanity was injured."

"Of course. It isn't what I'm used to."

"Injured but not killed," she said.

Chapter 10

IN NEED OF ANOTHER OPINION, she told Jack about Jason Bell and his teasing connections to the bombing case. "It's like a puzzle," she said, "with pieces mixed in from another puzzle."

"Where do you go from here?" he said.

"Try to get a warrant to look at Bell's bank account, if there is one. Track his movements over the last two weeks. See what I can find out about the surveillance footage from around the clinic on that night. The FBI's been running the show for a few days now, so they probably have it."

They were eating dinner at the little kitchen table, which had quickly won out over the larger dining-room table, and she poured them some more wine. "So what do you make of Bell?" she said. "Would you profile him as a bomber?"

Jack considered. "He was an angry man, according to his sister, and it isn't hard to see why. There's his Army experience—the death of a friend, and the death of innocence, seeing things no one is prepared to see, especially someone so young. Then the transition from a tight-knit, ordered, purposeful military culture—

whatever horrors it exposes you to—back to civilian life with all its looseness and alienation. And his girlfriend breaking up with him. And of course the inaction of the VA, once he'd decided to seek their help. When he admitted his problems to himself, he might have felt a little hope for the first time, which their denial dashed. You could say he was a bomb waiting to explode."

"That could also be the profile of a suicide, couldn't it?"

"Yes. One thing suicide accomplishes is to obliterate the world."

"What about his coming here?" she said. "How does that play into either scenario?"

"It connects most directly to suicide, I think. The fact he wanted to see General Gates in person suggests he'd invested him with a special authority—maybe imagined him as someone who could triumph over the VA. The offer of a campaign job—assuming there was one—might have fallen short of his inflated expectations, and once the disappointment sank in, he would have felt on his own again, only more so."

"So he lingers here," she said, "drinking and spiraling down to that moment in the car on the dead-end road. But why there?"

"Could have been spur of the moment," Jack said. "He may have been driving around, with no plan, and noticed the road leading into woods, into solitude, and it was a kind of trigger."

Cynthia left it at that, with the puzzle pieces still resisting connection. Jack's suicide hypothesis, unlike Jeff's, didn't hinge on remorse over the deaths in the explosion. And if Bell had been a bomb waiting to explode, as Jack had said, nothing she'd learned about him pointed to the clinic as a target for his rage. Still, she couldn't escape the feeling that his being here when the bomb went off wasn't just a coincidence.

At eleven, before following Jack to bed, she turned on the local news. The FBI announcement Ashley Hunter had mentioned was the lead story. The FBI spokesperson, a balding, jowly man named Archer, said the autopsy report on Kristen Gates and the details of the crime scene indicated she was having an abortion.

"Who arranged it?" a reporter asked.

"We don't know," Archer said. "Dr. Beatty, the attending physician, told no one about it, as far as we've been able to determine. Ms. Gates could have arranged it with him herself."

"Who's the father?" another reporter asked.

"Nothing yet on that, either. But our primary focus is finding the person or persons who planted the bomb."

The next story was a brief interview with Sam Spencer, the boorish candidate who'd referred to Gates as General Jellyfish. Asked for his reaction to Kristen Gates's death, he put on a sober face and said, "It's a great tragedy, and my thoughts and prayers are with the General and his wife. But we shouldn't forget all the other tragedies that took place at that clinic. Every day there for years, doctors sworn to do no harm killed innocent, unborn children."

He'd walked right up to the edge, Cynthia thought, by implying a rough justice had been served, and in his heartlessness there was a kind of provocation to more violence.

❁ ❁ ❁

Gates quit the race, as Ashley Hunter had said he would. Before she and Jack sat down to dinner with Sally at the farm house, the three of them watched him do it on the evening news. Standing with soldierly erectness on the walk outside his North Hill office, his gray suit and dark red tie like a uniform of mourning, the creases in his lived-in face seeming to have deepened even further, he said, "Some have advised me to end our campaign, saying our loss of support is irreversible. Others, including my staff, have urged me to fight on, believing our supporters will come back to us. I choose to think the latter, out of respect for the discernment and compassion of the American people. But before receiving any advice, I'd made my decision. It wasn't really a decision, but a necessity. Frankly, I lack the will to continue. Service to your country is a high responsibility, and I would not wish to seek it half-heartedly. So I leave the field to those with the dedication to pursue it—and, I hope, a keen awareness of its noble purpose." He then thanked his campaign workers and staff, with particular words of praise for Ashley Hunter, who stood solemnly to one side.

Sally, dabbing at her eyes with a tissue, said, "I guess what he said about a noble purpose was directed at that horrible Spencer. I hope people get the point."

Whether they did or not, Cynthia was too preoccupied with Jason Bell to pay much attention. Over the next few days she and Jeff managed to put him in the North Hill state liquor store but nowhere else: he'd been like a ghost moving through the town. They also checked with Larry, the tech, to see what he'd found.

"Only Bell's prints on the gun," he said, "and of course there are unknown prints on the car—it'd be unusual if there weren't."

"You got the tire impressions, right?" Jeff said.

Larry gave him the slow burn. "You want 'em? Maybe you could use 'em for a wall decoration."

After talking to Larry they went to see Charles. He was at his work under the bright lights cutting into a skull, the face beneath it hidden by a pulled-back flap of skin. When he turned off the little saw, Cynthia said, "We were wondering if you'd had a chance to do the blood work on Bell."

"The suicide?" Charles said. "Yes, I'll be sending you the report shortly, but the gist is he was drunk as a skunk. Blood alcohol point eighteen. It's a miracle he was able to shoot himself."

"You think he was too drunk to do it?"

"No, not necessarily. But he would have been challenged."

"Any thoughts on the downward angle of the bullet?"

"Extreme. But inebriation could account for that. With a little luck, he could have missed himself entirely."

Back on their floor, she went alone to see Roger, since Jeff couldn't help antagonizing him. When he said "Yes?" to her knock, she took it as an invitation and opened the door. He was fingering his phone, from which came blooping noises. Looking up in surprise, he swiftly lowered the phone out of sight.

"Sorry," she said.

"No, that's..."

The picture of him with his wife and kids, she noticed, was no longer on the filing cabinet. In its place were separate photos of his sons, both of whom had inherited his pasty complexion and sulky lower lip.

"How are your boys doing?" she said.

"Fine, from what I can tell," he said, as if he wished his absence made a greater difference.

"How about yourself?"

He reddened. "Oh, you know. Still getting used to..."

"Takes time," she said.

"Yeah."

"So what do you hear about the clinic case? The feds making any progress?"

His eyes, having gone a bit moony, snapped back into focus. "Oh, they might have gotten a lead on the dynamite—some was stolen from a blasting site in West Virginia. Other than that, not much."

Expeditions to find dynamite, she thought, could explain Bell's ghostliness in North Hill. "I assume they've been looking at surveillance tapes."

Roger nodded. "Seems like whoever did it was lucky about avoiding cameras."

"Or good at it. Reason I stopped by, Jason Bell, the apparent suicide we've been investigating, was part of a bomb squad in the Army."

"He was?" Roger said unhappily. On the wall behind him was a framed photo of Sheriff Sampson, who'd made it abundantly clear she was to have nothing to do with the case.

"So maybe there's a tie-in to the bombing," she said. "We'd like to check Bell's financials, to see if there's anything suspicious."

"Lemme get back to you on that," said Roger.

A hour later, he showed up at her desk with a hangdog expression. Jeff, who'd seen him approaching, joined them.

Ignoring Jeff, Roger said, "I'm sorry, Cynthia, but I can't support a warrant. There just isn't enough cause."

"Bomb guy shows up, bomb goes off," Jeff chimed in. "That doesn't strike you as a teeny bit suspicious?"

Roger glared at him. "I've made my decision," he said.

"We'll run it by Sampson, then," Jeff said.

"No point. I already—" Roger stopped himself.

Jeff grinned.

Blushing, Roger told her again he was sorry and retreated.

"One of these days you're going to push too hard," Cynthia said.

"Well, if I do, I'll just say, 'Please, please, Captain Bullock, whatever you do, don't promote me to sergeant!' And if that doesn't work, I still have you for insurance."

"Don't count on me. You just saw how much influence I have."

She spent the afternoon finishing up some paperwork, her least favorite part of the job, and as she was preparing to leave, the phone rang. It was Sampson.

"Westbrook," he said, "I need you to come to the North Hill police station. Pronto." He hung up.

She assumed this had to do with her request for a warrant. Not content to reject it through Roger, he wanted to give her a proper dressing down in person. But when she arrived at the station, Sampson, though looking grim, merely introduced her to Archer, the agent she'd seen on TV. Archer shook her hand and invited her to look at a pin board filled with pictures of faces, some of them from driver's licenses, and others taken outside the clinic before its destruction. Three of the latter caught her eye: Henry Arnold,

George Brown, and Rachel Dudley.

"We started with the clinic protestors," Archer said, "identifying them, gathering information about them, interviewing them. So far we've talked to forty-two people. Most we've dismissed as suspects for various reasons, but we remain interested in these three." He pointed to Arnold, Brown, and Rachel. "We had them in for questioning. They claim they were at Arnold's residence on the night of the bombing, but they only have each other for alibis. I understand you've met them."

"Yes, sir. I saw them with Steve Williams—the officer who died—a couple of weeks ago. A neighbor was concerned that Brown might have some sort of hold over Arnold."

"Does he?"

"Not that we could tell."

"Any impression about whether they'd be capable of violence to promote their cause?"

"I really can't see them doing that."

"Why not?"

"Hard to explain, but the two men are so focused on Rachel—Ms. Dudley." She remembered Arnold's gun collection, but decided not to mention it. Rachel, in her condition, didn't need the FBI breathing down her neck any more than it already had.

"Could she have inspired them to commit violence?" Archer said.

"No, sir, definitely not. She's just a timid kid. But there is something else. A suicide we've been investigating—"

"That'll be all, Westbrook," Sampson interrupted.

"Was a bomb expert in the Army, and came here to see Gates," she finished.

Archer pulled out his notebook. "You have more?" he said.

Conscious of Sampson's angry stare, she told him what she knew and also described Jack's view of Bell. "It might be a good idea," she said, "to see if he received any money in the last few months."

"We'll look into it. Thank you, detective."

As she was walking out, Sampson caught up with her. "You crossed the line, Westbrook," he said in a lowered voice. "That's twice now. I know Williams' girlfriend found out about his death from you. You're testing my patience. Do I make myself clear?"

"Yes, sir."

As he peeled away, it occurred to her she'd done the sort of thing she'd just cautioned Jeff against. But at least Bell was in the mix now.

Chapter 11

SHE TOLD JEFF ABOUT HER run-in with Sampson, and they decided to lay low for a few days, easy enough to do since they didn't have any leads. But it was difficult to put the bombing case out of her mind. For one thing, the dead called her back to it. Midweek she arranged with Amber Warren for her brother's body to be shipped to Dumfries, and on Friday afternoon she attended Steve's funeral. Jack had offered to go with her, but she told him it wasn't necessary, since she planned to slip in and out. "I'll just be there to swell the attendance," she said. "They don't know me." He assented to this in his discreet way, looking as if he understood more than he let on.

The funeral was held in a rural Baptist church, one of those century-old white wooden structures with a squat steeple. When she arrived, the dark clouds behind it accentuated the whiteness, giving it a kind of archetypal quality as a bastion against evil, or, as they case may be, a whited sepulcher. She'd heard that cops were coming from all the northern counties, and the parking lot at the back was filled up with cop cars and motorcycles. An usher directed her out of the lot to a side street, where she parked on the grassy shoulder. She made her way uncomfortably across a strip of lawn in her seldom worn low-heel pumps, and as she was going past a side building linked to the church by a covered walk, Shannon appeared in its doorway and came out and hugged her.

"Saw you through the window," Shannon said. She was wearing a pale yellow dress, not bridal white but not black either. "Come in and meet the family."

Reluctantly, Cynthia followed her inside, where a small crowd eyed the stranger in their midst.

"Everybody," Shannon announced, "this is Cynthia. She's the one who told me about Steve when the police wouldn't." She introduced Steve's parents, grandmother and two brothers, and the wife and little boy of one brother, and her own parents and sister, leaving the naming of the various aunts, uncles, and cousins to the married brother. Everyone was somber, even the little boy, who was too young to understand what was happening. Steve's mother looked stricken, her eyes red and downcast. The brother's wife placed an arm around Shannon as if trying to keep her in the family, though today would mark the end of that association, at least as marriage would have formalized it. Once again, Cynthia witnessed the blighting effect of an untimely, violent death.

A man opened a side door and invited the family to use the walkway. She left through the door she'd come in, went around to the chapel entrance, and found a seat near the back among the uniformed cops. The tall, clear-glass windows, three on each side, were raised, but it was a warm day made warmer by all the bodies crammed into the relatively narrow space, and people were fanning themselves with the programs. When the pianist stopped playing, the minister, an energetic little man in a dark suit, launched into a theological explanation of the afterlife, describing Heaven as a "holding place" for the souls of the saved that on judgment day would be reunited with their restored bodies. As he spoke, a light rain began to fall, sending a breeze through the open windows, and people lowered their programs. The feeling of relief was palpable, despite the gravity of the occasion. "Some believe the soul sleeps until judgment," the minister said, "but I don't accept that. I believe the Lord desires bliss for us, from the moment our first earthly life ends."

She thought of Steve in bliss waiting to enter his recreated body and live forever with his loved ones, providing they were saved too. That was the iron in the story. This little minister with his high-pitched voice and disarming, gap-toothed smile seemed nothing like the combative, self-righteous Brown, but he'd likely agree with Brown that some souls—probably a great many—would be spending eternity in a lake of fire, and among them would be the women who'd had abortions, maybe even the rape and incest victims.

Aside from that qualification, however, the story of eternal bliss was a shield against despair. *O, death, where is thy sting? O, grave, where is thy victory?* Without it the prospect was bleak. Steve gone forever, her mother and Bill too, no one spared. Erasure. And where did that leave her? With love and work, the chief components of happiness according to Dr. Freud. Her mother and then Sally and Bill had supplied the love, and now Jack. And after a period of indecisiveness, she'd found the work she was meant to do. Catching criminals. That was the iron in her story. But she saw it as an aspect of pushing back against chaos, which had first made itself known to her in her mother lying dead in a pool of blood. Yet whether chaos could be successfully resisted seemed more and more an open question, in this hateful and brutal time.

They stood and sang "The Old Rugged Cross." Then people came forward and talked about Steve. The North Hill police chief praised him as a model officer. The brothers and a few friends remembered his athletic prowess in school and some of the silly things he'd done that in the telling made him live again as a particular human being with quirks and foibles, and so briefly overcame sorrow. After this there was another hymn, and it was over. She got out before the cops could climb on their motorcycles and lead the procession to the cemetery. Fortunately, the rain had stopped, leaving behind its accidental gift of coolness.

Not long after the funeral the bombing case made itself felt again. "There's a rumor popping up online," Jeff told her, "that Gates was the one who knocked up his daughter. You think it's politics?"

"Don't see why it would be," she said. "He's not in the race. But it reminds me of what happened to John McCain, in his first run for president."

"I was a mere babe then. Enlighten me."

"McCain lost the South Carolina primary because some dirty tricksters spread rumors about him. One was that he'd fathered his adopted daughter, a Bangladesh orphan."

"Dark skinned girl?"

"Yep. In fact, the fliers described her as a Negro."

"Okay, that's really bad, but this is even worse—whoever did it."

And then things took a completely unexpected and even more disturbing turn. The feds, having called Arnold and his guests in for a second, more aggressive interview, showed up at his house with a search warrant; but before they reached the door, Arnold appeared brandishing a rifle and forced them to back off. They tried to call him, and when no one answered, they set up a blockade halfway down the drive.

When she got word of this, she bypassed Roger and went to Sampson's office on the top floor. His secretary said he was at the North Hill station, so she drove there. Since her last visit, the main room had been converted almost entirely into an FBI command center, with men and women in civvies at most of the desks. Sampson, his back to her, was talking to Archer and another man, and she reached him before he was aware of her.

"Sir," she said, causing him to whirl around at the sound of her voice, "I'm worried about Rachel—the young woman in the house. The strain can't be good for—"

"Not your problem, Westbrook," he said.

"Hello, again, detective," said Archer. "I share your worry. We'd certainly like to get her out of there, but so far they aren't talking to us."

"With all due respect, sir," she said to Archer, "I hope you don't plan to prod them into it by cutting the electricity. We've had some warm days lately, and Rachel might not fare well without air conditioning."

The other man, who was swarthy and bearded, nodded. "That's a good point," he said. "We'll leave it on."

"John Bertrand, our negotiating expert," Archer said.

Bertrand shook her hand. "Bill's told me about you, Detective Westbrook. I'd like to know your impressions of these folks."

She repeated everything she'd told Archer in their first meeting, adding to it Jack's speculations about Rachel and her companions. When she finished, he said, "Thanks, very helpful. But you don't they think they did it, is that right? Their resistance hasn't changed your mind?"

"No, sir," she said. "I understand they were subjected to a fairly intense interrogation. So Arnold may have thought he was protecting Rachel from arrest. And Brown might be afraid to challenge him—I don't know the dynamics."

"That makes two of us. Look, if you think of anything else, please give me a call. I'd like your number too."

They exchanged cards. Walking to the door, she glanced back and saw Sampson talking, his face a mask of professional composure. Maybe her potential usefulness to Bertrand had afforded her some protection.

This proved to be true, seemingly. She heard nothing from either Sampson or his reluctant henchman Roger. Meanwhile, the standoff continued, and because of its ties to the clinic bombing, it received extensive media coverage. TV crews, restricted to the roadside, captured zoom images through blurry foliage of Arnold foolishly appearing in a downstairs window with a rifle in his hand, and of the various law-enforcement types—agents and deputies and U.S. Marshals—standing idly behind the line of cars and jeeps, like cops at a picnic.

Watching one of these reports with Jack, she said, "Did Arnold surprise you, chasing the feds off?"

"Everything about human nature surprises me," he said. "I think that's why I went into psychology, to make up for my inadequacy. As you said, Arnold may have thought he was protecting the girl, but I wonder if he wasn't also keeping her to himself. And maybe trying to impress his father. The gun collecting would seem to be a gesture in that direction."

"Even though his father's dead."

"The people who matter to us never really die, do they?"

She thought of her mother. "No, they don't."

Four days after he'd asked for her number, Bertrand phoned her. "They finally took our call," he said. "Brown answered. I asked him to put Arnold on, since Arnold's the one with the gun, and I could hear them talking, but no go."

"So who's running the show?" Cynthia said. "Arnold or Brown?"

"That's the million-dollar question. Arnold obviously initiated things, and he's still a free agent, judging by his refusal to come to the phone. But Brown seems to have some power too."

"Why? Because he answered the phone?"

"More because of the request he made, which seems to come from him. He asked us to send in someone to talk things over. A specific someone: you."

"Me? Why me?"

"He said he trusts you. But I'm not necessarily proposing you do it. It's risky."

"He invited me, so the risk would seem fairly low. And it's certainly worth a try if it can help end the standoff. Count me in."

"Take a moment," Bertrand said.

"No need."

"All right. I'll call your sheriff, and if he agrees, I'll call Brown to set it up."

A half hour later, Bertrand phoned to say Brown would be expecting her at nine the next morning. "He wanted the meeting today," he said, "but I told him you weren't available. Never a good idea to comply instantly with a demand—you don't want them to feel in charge."

She thought about telling Jack, who would likely have some helpful things to say, but who would also worry, and in the end she kept it to herself.

Chapter 12

ACROSS THE ROAD FROM THE news crews and satellite trucks there were maybe thirty people holding signs. One of these read, "Baby Killers the Real Criminals!"—a sentiment that didn't take into account the actual fate of Kristen's fetus, or the deaths of Kristen, Dr. Beatty, and Steve. She recognized the little group of aging men who'd dumped baby-doll parts in the paths of women patients. The standoff had given them something to do after the destruction of the clinic.

She showed her badge to the guards and drove down to the blockade, where the cops seemed to have lost their holiday mood. Instead of socializing, most of them were staring at the big house fifty yards down the hill, or staring at its new feature: an American flag hanging on a short pole in the circular garden. She parked off the drive a few yards uphill from the line and searched for Bertrand. He was with Archer behind one of the sheriff cars.

The first thing he said was, "I should've phoned you, but I got distracted. We need to call it off."

"Anything to do with that flag?" she said.

"Everything. Half an hour ago, some armed men came out of the house and put it up. We think during the night they must have crossed the pond behind the house. We weren't surveilling heavily there, because of the pond."

"Who are the armed men?"

"We're trying to identify them," Archer said. "They were wearing military-style clothing, so they could be from a local militia group called the Defenders, as in defenders of the Constitution, although up until now its members haven't given us any trouble. They mainly go out in the woods and do training exercises."

"Have you heard from anybody in the house this morning?" she said.

"Brown," Bertrand said.

"And?"

"I told him you weren't coming in unless the men left. He said they were Arnold's friends, and it would be all right. I got the impression he didn't think he could do anything about them."

"How many of them are there?" she asked him.

"Three put up the flag. But there could be others."

"That's something I can find out," she said.

"It's too risky," Bertrand said. "We don't know what they want."

"I can find that out too. Look, I'm here, and I'm willing. The most important thing is that this ends peacefully."

Bertrand looked at Archer, who said, "It would be a help."

"I'll need to call your captain," Bertrand said to her.

"As I'm sure you're aware," she said, "Sheriff Sampson doesn't exactly appreciate my participation in this case. Roger—Captain Bullock—will consult with him, and the changed circumstances might give him an excuse to be less accommodating this time. He allowed it when there was already an element of risk, and I've stated my desire to do it. That should be enough."

After a few moments, Bertrand said, "All right. So long as you're taking responsibility for it."

"I am."

Archer said, "Have your meeting outside, if you can. We've got snipers posted. And let's get you a vest."

"I think that would send the wrong signal," she said.

"Wear one anyway."

He called someone over, who fetched a vest from a van. She put it on, handed Archer her gun, and began walking down the drive. It was another perfect spring day. Clouds raced across the blue sky and birds twittered in the trees. As she reached the circular garden, a breeze lifted and unfurled the flag, incongruously evoking a sense of normalcy, school grounds and ball games and the Fourth.

The front door opened and a man stepped onto the portico. He had a buzz cut and a long, narrow face. He was wearing camouflage pants, a black t-shirt, and a gear vest. Strapped to his right thigh was a holstered gun.

"Cynthia Westbrook," she said. "Sheriff's investigator."

"Keep coming," he said.

"Your name?"

He smiled faintly. "Neil Carson. Patriot at large."

"Can they talk out here?"

"They're ready for you inside."

Having no choice, she entered and saw two other men in similar garb further back in the hall. They were both hefty and full-bearded, with AK-47s slung across their chests. The chief difference between them was that one had painted his face green and black. Behind them on the Persian runner sat an inflated yellow raft, probably what they'd put the flag and their weapons in, and maybe their clothes.

"Cynthia Westbrook," she said to them.

"Jack Hammer," Face Paint said, and his companion let out a low, raspy chuckle. Tweedledum and Tweedledee, the sinister version.

"I suspect the FBI has all our names by now," Carson said. "Turn around, please, and put your hands on the door. Sorry, but I need to pat you down."

"I'll do it if you don't want to," Face Paint said, and Tweedledee chuckled again.

Carson, ignoring them, moved his hands lightly down her body.

"Why are you here?" she said to him. "Are you against abortion?"

"Nope. For it, actually. I don't like the idea of the government telling anyone what to do. We're here for Henry. We've known him a long time, from the shooting range. He's our brother in arms."

"Nothing to do with this," she said.

"You can turn around now."

When she did, he said, "Americans have the right to defend themselves against an illegitimate authority. That's what Henry's doing."

"No, it isn't."

He gestured toward the parlor. "They're in there."

She went in. Like last time, Brown, Arnold, and Rachel were sitting in chairs drawn up around the coffee table. Rachel smiled at her, but the smile was less radiant than before and vanished quickly. Maybe Sleeping Beauty was waking up. She hoped so. Her private agenda was to take Rachel with her, or short of that, to lessen the danger for her as much as possible. She smiled back, then glanced at the others. Arnold, chubby man-child, sat with shoulders slumped and head down, but Brown returned her gaze. He seemed strangely cheerful under the circumstances.

"Glad you could join us," he said, and gestured at the empty chair across from him.

Sitting down, she noticed the coffee table held a tray with cups and a carafe. Hospitality seemed somewhat beside the point, even a little absurd, like the flag fluttering in the garden.

"Would you like some coffee?" Rachel asked politely in her

trailer-park twang.

To establish a connection, Cynthia said, "Yes, thanks."

"Cream and sugar?"

"Black's fine, thank you."

As she took the offered cup, she stared deep into Rachel's greenish eyes, trying to convey something of her purpose.

"So, Cynthia," Brown said, "what is your view of our… situation?"

"It's time to end it," she said. "Past time. You were already playing with fire, but now with these armed men here, the fire's out of control."

"They were a surprise, weren't they, Brother Henry?" Brown said to Arnold.

Arnold didn't respond.

"There's also Rachel's health," she said. "This is hard on her and her baby."

"Yes," Brown said, looking at Arnold rather than at Rachel. "Brother Henry, is there something you'd like to ask?"

Arnold, head still down, let out a shuddery breath. "What will happen to Rachel?"

Skirting the issue of what would happen to *him*, Cynthia said, "I don't see how she could be held responsible for any of this—I'll certainly vouch for her. And as for the bombing, if she had nothing to do with it, she has nothing to worry about."

"Innocent people go to jail," Arnold said.

"True. It happens. But the FBI doesn't just want to put somebody in jail. They want to stop whoever caused the explosion from doing it again. The far greater threat to Rachel is the one she's facing here."

Brown put his hand on Arnold's shoulder. "All right, Brother Henry?"

Arnold reacted with a barely perceptible nod.

Was that it? Had she succeeded? She put the cup down. "So let's tell your militia friends it's over," she said, "and walk out together."

"We will," Brown said. "But there's something I must do first."

A premonition like a sharp stab stopped her from asking what.

"Sinner that I am," Brown said, "God chose me as his instrument. He arranged all this so the whole nation would know of my witness. But there is one more thing He has directed me to do. Tell Mr. Bertrand to send a television reporter to interview me, someone from the national news, and after they broadcast it, we'll come out."

She had an inkling now of what must have happened. Brown might have been intimidated at first by Arnold's defiance of the agents, but he'd soon realized it shone a spotlight on him, and at some point, probably early on, he'd come up with the idea of being on TV—or God had, the God he'd made in his own image. He'd then started nudging Arnold toward surrender, which is where she came in. However self-involved and insensitive Brown might be, he wasn't stupid; he'd taken note of her concern for Rachel and surmised correctly he could enlist her to help him with Arnold. Even the militia boys hadn't deterred him from carrying out his plan. In fact, they'd played into it by creating another threat for her to bring up.

"It's too risky to string this out," she said to Brown. "You can do your interview when it's over."

"Can I?" Brown said. "Would the police permit it? Would reporters be interested? No, it needs to be here."

She studied Brown's knobby, impervious face, a little flushed now with excitement, and concluded it was pointless to try to dissuade him. He was lost in his hall of mirrors. "I'll pass along your condition," she said, "but I'd like Rachel to leave with me, for her protection."

Rachel gave her a startled look.

"I can't allow that," Brown said.

"It's not up to you."

"I need Rachel by my side. It's part of God's plan."

"A loving God wouldn't want this," she said, looking at Rachel.

"You can't speak for God," Brown said. "Your understanding is darkened."

Cynthia stood and held out her hand. "Rachel, please come with me."

In his tenderly possessive way Brown brushed a strand of blond hair from the girl's brow. "Just a little longer," he said.

"For your baby's sake," Cynthia said.

Eyes lowered, Rachel shook her head.

Cynthia tried another tactic. "Henry," she said, using Arnold's first name to lend herself a kind of maternal authority, "I know you want to keep Rachel safe. If she feels she can't leave, the best way to help her is tell your friends to give themselves up."

Meeting her eyes for the first time, Arnold said, "They won't listen to me. I didn't invite them here."

"If that's true, then give yourself up, and they won't have any reason to stay."

"But it's only a little longer," he said, echoing Brown, though with a melancholy that was his own.

"That's right, Brother Henry," Brown said. He regarded Cynthia with a cold, tight-lipped smile. "Brother Henry told me you'd been in the news, so I looked you up on his computer, and I read about your mother. She was young and unmarried when she had you. God bless her. Many in her place would have gone to a butchery."

This too, she thought, was behind his requesting her.

"Why did she let you live, Cynthia?" he said. "Did you believe your life was sacred?"

"She had me because she wanted me," Cynthia said. "And she

would never have abandoned me, like you have your own children."

"Are you finished with your coffee?" Rachel asked as if she hadn't heard any of this. When Cynthia didn't answer, she moved the cup back to the tray, stood, and picked up the tray.

"Rachel," Cynthia said again.

Silently, Rachel left the room through a side door. Without speaking to Brown or Arnold again, Cynthia got up too and went out into the hall.

Carson was waiting for her there.

"Can we talk?" she said.

"I don't see it would make any difference."

"Please hear me out anyway."

He considered. "All right."

"But not here."

"Then follow me."

He led her to the room Steve Williams had described, the one with the guns. There were more than she'd imagined, in wall-to-wall cabinets and waist-high display cases, everything scented with the not unpleasant smell of gun oil emanating from a work table at one end. "First time Henry showed me all this," Carson said, his eyes roaming the treasures, "I was bowled over. It's the history of our country. We exist because of these weapons."

"Henry doesn't think about it that way," she said. "To him it's about remembering his father, or being like his father. He's not one of you."

Carson shrugged. It was an ambiguous gesture, meaning either he didn't share her opinion or didn't care.

"You weren't invited to the standoff," she said.

"But we haven't been un-invited."

She thought about challenging him on that, but he could counter, with some justice, that Arnold didn't want things to end. "What do you hope to accomplish?" she said.

"Remind the government of the constitution. And of what will happen if they try to subvert it."

"Viva la revo-loosh-eon," someone said behind her. She turned and saw Face Paint in the doorway with Tweedledee peering over his shoulder like a second head on the same body. Face Paint was holding a bottle of liquor.

"Where'd you get that?" Carson said.

"We liberated it from Henry's liquor cabinet."

"Well, put it back."

"Henry won't mind. He's our buddy."

"Now," Carson said. "We need clear heads."

The two men disappeared from the doorway.

"It isn't just your life you're risking," she said; "it's the girl's."

"She turned you down."

"Brown controls her."

"So you say."

She was struck anew by the profound irrationality of the situation. Carson, Arnold, and Brown had entirely different motives for wanting it to continue. All they shared was a slender hold on reality.

"The government doesn't want your guns," she said. "There's no vast conspiracy at work."

"What I'd expect you to say," Carson replied. "You're part of the system. You've been co-opted."

He said this so calmly, he might have been talking about the weather. To get under his skin a little, she said, "And you've been co-opted by a fantasy. Come out with me and put this behind you."

Carson, seemingly unperturbed, gestured toward the door. "Shall we?" he said.

When they passed the parlor, she saw only Brown, his reddish hair further enflamed by the window light. He was reading his Bible, or pretending to, and didn't look up. A show of piety intended for her, she supposed. Arnold must have followed Rachel into the kitchen, trying to make the most of their dwindling time together. What did Rachel feel toward him? Or could she allow herself to feel anything?

Behind her, she heard kissing noises. She turned and saw Face Paint, his lips puckered, standing in front of the raft with Tweedledee.

"This isn't a game," she said. "It isn't chasing each other around in the woods."

"I wouldn't mind chasing you," Face Paint said, and Tweedledee chuckled.

Carson opened the door.

"You know you can't count on them," she said to him.

Doubt flickered across his face. But he said, "Give my regards to the government."

Chapter 13

WALKING BACK UP THE DRIVE, Cynthia surveyed the barricade from the perspective of those in the house. It was daunting. A small army of cops, their upper bodies visible above the hoods and trunks of the vehicles, was watching her. She imagined how it would feel to be in the sights of all those guns, and the thought made her shiver in the warm sun.

Bertrand and Archer were waiting for her. She briefed them, and when she finished, Bertrand said, "That certainly complicates things. I'd prefer to deal with one set of fanatics at a time."

"Sorry I didn't get all the names," she said.

"We got them from the photos taken this morning," Archer said. "As we suspected, they're members of the Defenders, but they're a fringe group within it—a fringe of the fringe. The Defenders leader just disavowed them on the phone."

"Carson, the one who seems to be in charge," she said, "I think he may have the same general strategy as Brown: resist, make your point, then surrender. But I don't know about his buddies. I wouldn't count on them to follow their leader."

"Obviously, we can't allow a real news crew to go in," Bertrand said. "We'll have to use agents in disguise. It's also problematic whether any of the networks would air the footage, or air it in a way that would satisfy Brown. So I'll try to talk him around before we meet his demand."

As he spoke, he stared uneasily at the flag, which only added to her unease.

❀ ❀ ❀

That evening she chose again not to say anything to Jack about the standoff, but he brought it up.

"I heard some militia types have joined Arnold and his guests," he said.

"Right," she said.

"And a sheriff's investigator met with them all."

"That would be me," she said.

"When I got home, I saw TV coverage of you coming back from the house."

His voice had gone quiet and calm. *This is Jack being pissed*, she thought. *Really pissed.*

"Why didn't you tell me?" he said.

"I didn't know about the militia guys until I arrived."

"But you were already planning to go in."

"Yeah," she said. "I didn't want to worry you."

"Maybe I could have given you some advice."

Let him get it out. "What would you have advised?"

"That you communicate with them by telephone, because your judgment might be too clouded for a face to face."

"How so?"

"You're personally involved in this case. Steve Williams' death has affected you, and you were worried about Rachel even before she was caught up in the investigation. Maybe you identify her a little bit with your mother."

Her first impulse was to strike back at him for questioning her professionalism. But she didn't want to discuss Steve with him, and he'd been right before about her losing her objectivity and with it her cop's instinct for danger. Her second impulse was to deny his suggestion concerning her mother because, she realized, there might be something to it. For one thing, Brown's comment on her mother had struck home despite their disagreement about abortion. So she hung fire.

"Jack," she said, "I was aware of the risk, but I decided it was worth it to try and get Rachel out. Whoever I may identify her with, she's an innocent girl in trouble."

He was silent for a while. "Okay, I can see that. But I'd appreciate it if you'd let me help, when I can be of help."

"Even if I don't listen to you in the end?"

"Yes."

"All right, then."

"My replacement at Quantico, by the way, called this morning to consult about the militia men."

"Oh? What did you learn? All I know is they're in a group called the Defenders."

"They're all loners, to a degree—which fits the general profile of militia members. Carson, the oldest, is divorced. Last year his ex-wife remarried and moved out of state with their children. The other two, Aldridge and Watts, have never been married. Aldridge lives with his mother, and Watts has had some trouble with the law: unpaid speeding tickets, public drunkenness, and stalking."

"Watts sounds like the loosest cannon," she said, thinking he must be Face Paint.

"That was my replacement's opinion too. But I told him I'd be equally concerned, or more concerned, about Carson. According to the leader of the Defenders, he's always pressing them to do things, not all of it legal. He's not in it for the camaraderie of a shared delusion about gun confiscation or a UN takeover, or whatever it is they imagine precisely. He wants to take action. He's a true believer."

Jack had cooled down now, or rather heated up. The warmth had returned to his voice.

"So how did it feel," she said, "to be doing your old job?"

"Not bad. But it didn't make me miss it. I prefer the new one."

"And what about your new living arrangement? You prefer it to the old one too?"

"I do."

They were sitting on the couch, and she leaned over and kissed him. "Is this one of the reasons?" she said.

"It is," he said, and kissed her back.

A few minutes later they moved to the bedroom and engaged in some fairly vigorous love making. Afterward, she said, "I guess that qualifies as make-up sex."

"Does it?"

"Now, doctor. Honesty is a two-way street."

He found her hand beneath the sheet. "It's just that I don't want to lose you."

"I know. I feel the same way. It's a good thing, don't you think?"

"Yes."

They lay for a time silently in the dark, and Jack, as he usually did after such occasions, drifted off. His hand relaxed in hers, and his breathing became deep and rhythmic.

Still wound up from the day's events, she got out of bed, slipped on her robe, and went into the den. She pulled a rocker up to the TV and surfed the news channels with the volume low, seeing if she could find out anything more about the standoff. Archer appeared on one channel, admitting with a poker face to inadequate surveillance. "Not that we had any idea," he said, "a militia group might join in. Our investigation has nothing to do with the Second Amendment or federal oversight or anything like that."

On another channel she happened upon a breaking story about Kristen Gates. The father of Kristen's child, also a student at William and Mary, had revealed himself to the police. Interviewed by the station's reporter, he proved to be something of a surprise. He was a slender young black man with dreadlocks but an otherwise preppy look—dark-frame glasses and a blue sweater over a collared white shirt. "Kristen and I weren't really romantic," he said. "It was more of a friendship. We liked to hang out together and talk. But one night at a party we both had too much to drink, and it happened. When she found out she was pregnant, she told me she didn't want the baby. I offered to help her pay for an abortion, but she said she'd take care of it. And that's the last we talked about it, or talked much at all, really. After exams, she left to help her dad with his campaign."

"Why didn't you immediately go to the police?" the interviewer asked.

"I was afraid, I guess. Plus I didn't know anything."

"What made you change your mind?"

"The terrible rumor about her and her father. Her parents were suffering enough already, and I didn't want my silence to add to their pain."

For some reason, watching this compassionate young man sparked a question: What if Kristen had been the bomber's real target? That would eliminate the coincidence of her being at the clinic when it was destroyed. On the other hand, it raised the question of why anyone would want to kill her. Her death had caused her father to withdraw from the race, to the benefit of his rivals in both parties, all of whom had been lagging behind him in the polls. Yet it was hard to imagine any of these people, even Sam Spencer, actually killing for political gain. As dirty as politics had become, she couldn't see it turning literally murderous.

Nevertheless, she decided to run the possibility by Jeff.

Chapter 14

JEFF HAD THE SAME PROBLEM with her idea that she did. "I know politicians are greedy, unprincipled, hypocritical scumsuckers," he said, "but would they actually kill to win?"

"Maybe it isn't a politician but a zealous underling."

"A zealous psycho underling."

"Yes."

"Still, why not just leak the abortion to the press, or spread some lies? It would be less risky than blowing somebody up, and maybe just as effective. Like what you said about McCain. But suppose you're onto something—how would we go about finding this nut job? Six other campaigns are in the race, with any number of workers. Plus it isn't our case. We don't have the time or the say-so to look into all those people."

"I'm thinking it would involve someone in Gates's camp," she said, "someone Kristen felt she could tell her secret to."

"Okay, but Gates's campaign is defunct. All the workers are scattered by now. And it could also be someone outside the campaign, like a college friend who passed along the secret, or blabbed it to somebody who did."

"An outsider seems too far removed from the politics, which is all we've got for a motive—as tenuous as that is. Let's stick to people associated with the campaign. We could see what's available online—print stories, TV news, bios—and maybe something would stand out. At least that's doable in our spare time without Roger being any the wiser."

"I do like the idea of slipping one past Roger," Jeff said. "Why don't we divvy it up somehow? You could take the print, since you're the nerdy literate type, and I, being a normal, fun-loving person, could do the TV stuff."

They started their search on their phones at lunch time, and the task quickly came to seem hopeless. Before her death, Kristen had received little notice in the media. They gave up after a couple of hours and went back to the convenience-store robbery they'd been assigned. That evening, following Jack's delicious stuffed-peppers and squash-casserole dinner, which might have been a sort of addendum to the make-up sex, she searched some more, but without any more success, and went to bed. Then around two Jeff called.

She answered in the den.

"I was up with Angela," he said, "enjoying re-runs of *Gilligan's Island* and *Green Acres*. Did you know there are no black people in these shows? I can see it for a story about castaways. I mean, black folk are not too fond of water. Maybe it goes back to the slave ships."

"Jeff," she said, "it's the wee hours."

"Sorry. Guess I'm a little punchy. When I finally got Angela to sleep again, I did some more looking online and maybe found something. It's in the video, not the audio.   I'll send you the link."

The link was to a TV news story about a Gates rally in Roanoke. She muted the sound to concentrate on the images. Between shots of the reporter on the scene, there were around fifteen seconds of Gates speaking as his daughter and Ashley Hunter, among others, stood behind him on the platform. Halfway through this footage, Kristen whispered something in Ashley's ear, and Ashley, smiling, turned her head and whispered something back. It was an ordinary enough occurrence, but it hinted at a degree of intimacy between the two women.

She called Jeff.

"Well?" he said.

"I think I saw what you did. Also, it reminded me that Kristen's boyfriend, or friend, whatever, said she refused his help to pay for the abortion. If she didn't have the money herself, and didn't ask her father, where did it come from? Who would have had it?"

"Ah," Jeff said. "Your admirer?"

"A long shot, but maybe we should pursue it."

"How do we do that?"

"We could begin with the boyfriend. He might know more than he thinks he does."

Before going back to bed, she Googled Ashley Hunter and came across two campaign biographies of her. They were duplicates in all respects except one. Both said she'd attended a prestigious Richmond prep school and gone on to Harvard. Both referred to her previous campaign work, all of it for winners so far as Cynthia could remember. Both also said Politco had named her one of the "50 top politicos of 2010." The single difference was that one identified her as Gates's campaign manager, and the other as Spencer's. She'd moved on, apparently, soon after Gates made his announcement.

The next morning at work, she and Jeff fetched the boyfriend's name from the news and called the student office at William and Mary. They were told he'd withdrawn from his summer classes, so they got his home number, with a northern Pennsylvania area code, and talked to his mother, who gave them his cell number. When they finally reached him, Cynthia asked if Kristen had ever mentioned Ashley Hunter.

"No, ma'am," he said, "not that I recall."

"She ever talk about anyone in her father's campaign?"

"No, ma'am."

"She give you any sense of how she'd pay for the abortion, or arrange it?"

"No, ma'am. We didn't talk about it."

Jeff, who was on another phone, said, "She tell anyone she was pregnant beside you?"

"I'm pretty sure not. She was worried if word got out, it would hurt her dad's campaign. She swore me to secrecy."

"You keep your promise?"

"Yes, sir."

When they hung up, Jeff said, "Well, that was illuminating. Now what?"

"Hunter went to a private high school in Richmond. We could pay it a visit and see what we could find out about her."

"You mean, go rogue?"

"Just for a day."

"I'm in."

Chapter 15

WESTHAMPTON ACADEMY, ACCORDING TO ITS website, was a girls' school for pre-K through twelfth grade. It had been founded early in the previous century by two sisters, and from its fairly humble beginnings as a couple of wood-frame houses it had grown into a rather impressive number of tall brick buildings situated around a long green. The annual tuition was impressive too, from $16,000 in the lower grades to $22,000 in the upper. Cynthia and Jeff parked on the street across from the entrance and strolled up the brick walk to the white-columned administration building. After identifying themselves, they were ushered into the office of the headmistress, Amanda Riley, a slender, fiftyish woman in a dove gray jacket and pearl necklace, who offered them some tea.

Cynthia, declining for them, asked her if she remembered a former student named Ashley Hunter.

"Of course I remember Ashley," Ms. Riley said. "She was one of our standouts—top of her class, active in a number of clubs. She received our full high-school scholarship, and left here with a full scholarship to Harvard. I saw her just recently on the news, speaking on behalf of General Gates, that poor man. But why are you interested in her, if I may ask?"

"She's peripheral to something we're looking into," Cynthia said. "Can you tell me anything else about her?"

"Well, she came from an impoverished background—hence the scholarship. As I recall, she grew up in Bellwood, a little town about twenty miles south of Richmond. Someone, probably her mother, since there was no father in the picture, drove her here, that is until her senior year. That's when her mother died, horribly. When we learned about it, we sent word round to our girls' families, and one of them took her in."

"How did her mother die?" Cynthia said.

"Oh, it was quite sordid. She was murdered by a male friend after a night of drinking."

"And who was the family that took her in?"

"The Roxburys. Their daughter Miriam was in Ashley's class. I imagine it was a good arrangement for Miriam too, in the sense of giving her a positive role model. She was a shy girl, definitely not a joiner, and just an average student."

Cynthia, wondering whether a powerhouse like Ashley would in fact have been good for Miriam, made a note of the girl's name. "Do you have an address for Miriam Roxbury?"

"No, sorry. But her parents are still in Richmond. I see their names in the society news every now and then."

"What about Ashley—does she have family in the area?"

"I believe she was an only child, like Miriam. Other than that, I don't know anything."

When they got back in the car, Jeff did some Googling on his phone. "No other Hunters in Bellwood," he said. "But we may be in luck. There's a Miriam Roxbury in a Richmond apartment, and the address isn't too far from here. I'll punch it in."

Following the directions of the GPS voice—a rather flat female one, Jeff having deactivated Bugs without comment, which she chalked up as a victory for her side—they soon found Miriam Roxbury's complex. It was pricey, by the look of it: painted gray brick, dark green shutters, flowering fruit trees and other landscaping.

The woman who answered the door seemed about the right age. She was chunky and snub-nosed, with heavy eye makeup and bright red lipstick. Somewhat strangely, given the makeup, she was dressed in a blue jogging suit.

Cynthia introduced them and asked her if she'd gone to school with Ashley Hunter.

"Yeah," Miriam Roxbury said. "But I don't know her now."

"We'd be interested in what you remember about her."

Yielding to Cynthia's air of authority, Miriam let them inside her apartment, which was a mess. Articles of clothing lay strewn about, and take-out cartons and soda cans littered the coffee table and the kitchen counter. But the furnishings were expensive looking, a lot of Colonial replica stuff.

If Miriam was embarrassed, she didn't show it. After clearing off the sofa, she invited them to sit, and took a chair for herself.

"We understand," Cynthia said, "that Ms. Hunter lived with your family during your senior year at Westhampton Academy."

"Uh-huh," Miriam said.

"How did that work out?"

"All right," Miriam said, twisting her bright red mouth.

Something here, Cynthia thought. "The two of you get along okay?"

"I guess. It was a long time ago."

"Fifteen years. Not so long as all that."

Miriam shrugged.

Cynthia glanced at Jeff, her signal for him to employ his charm.

Smiling, he said, "So tell me, Miriam, what do you do?"

"I'm… between jobs at the moment. I was working as a dog groomer, but they had to lay some people off, and I've had trouble finding work."

"You would, these days," Jeff said, "the economy the way it is." He looked around. "Nice place. Hope you don't lose it."

"I won't. My parents pay for it."

"They sound like the right kind of parents to have."

"If you don't mind being told what to do."

Jeff chuckled. "I hear you. My mom's always sticking her nose in my business."

"They got me this place," Miriam said, "so I wouldn't look like somebody who'd flunked out of college. And they gave me a gym membership so I'd lose weight and find a boyfriend and get married. But I don't go to the gym. I just wear the clothes." She punctuated her confession with a breathy laugh.

"Well, at least you're not under their roof," Jeff said.

"Yeah. It's better than nothing. I still have to pick up before they come over. Otherwise I'd never hear the end of it."

"So how did they treat Ashley?" Jeff said. "They boss her around too?"

"Oh, no. They thought she was great. Perfect. Everything a daughter should be."

"That couldn't have been much fun for you. She make it worse, you know, by lording it over you?"

Miriam looked at him, looked away. "No, she wasn't like that. She said not to pay any attention to them. Because they had conventional minds."

"So the two of you were friends," Jeff said.

"For a while, I guess."

"Something happen?"

Miriam shifted uneasily. Her expression was one Cynthia had

seen before: shame contending with the desire to confess.

Jeff, who'd picked up on it too, said, "Sometimes it helps to get things off your chest."

Taking an audible breath, Miriam said, "My mom had this little black poodle named Princess, and Princess hated me. If I got too near Mom, she'd growl at me, and one time while I was watching TV, she bit me on the ankle for no reason at all. Ashley saw how she was around me, and when I told her about the bite, she said I should pay Princess back. Take her for a ride and leave her somewhere. So when we got the chance we put her in my car, or Ashley did—she was nice to Ashley—and we drove around for a while and came to this park."

When Miriam didn't continue, Jeff said, "You leave her there?"

Miriam shook her head. "Ashley got out with her and put her on the ground. Then she picked her up and got back in the car. She told me it was a test, a moral test, and I'd failed it. After that, she just sort of ignored me."

Cynthia, inserting herself into the conversation, said, "How did her ignoring you make you feel?"

"Like I deserved it," Miriam said. "What I'd wanted to do was a terrible thing."

"But you didn't want to do it," Cynthia said. "It was her idea, and you went along with it to please her. She manipulated you."

Miriam's surprised look suggested this was a possibility she hadn't considered. "But why?" she said.

"To make you feel the way you do. So don't let her."

When they were back in the car, Jeff said, "Dog groomer."

"Yeah. Probably not a coincidence. You gave your mom a hard time, by the way."

"I just enlisted her. Deputized her. It's really Denise's mom who keeps sticking her nose in. She doesn't approve of our child-rearing methods. We're either too lenient or too hard, depending on her mood."

"Well, based on what I've seen of little Angela, Denise is doing a great job."

Jeff grinned. "Gee, thanks."

Chapter 16

THINKING THE POLICE AND NOT the local sheriff would have handled the murder of Ashley's mother, she drove them to the Chesterfield County Police Department, located in an unattractive sprawl of low civic buildings. They told the desk cop they needed information on a Bellwood murder, and he summoned another cop who took them back to a computer and did a file search.

"Here we go," he said. "Alice Hunter. Lived in the Sans Souci apartments—or Sans Sucky as we call them. Subsidized housing, a real dump. The shit never lets up there. Fights, ODs, domestic abuse, you name it. Joseph Wornum, Hunter's boyfriend, strangled her with an extension cord. The daughter was in her room and heard them arguing, but she thought it was just another night at the OK Corral. The next morning she found her mother dead and Wornum passed out. He claimed not to remember anything, which is possible. He'd put away a lotta booze. Kind of surprising he had the wherewithal to strangle somebody, even if it was another drunk."

Jeff raised his eyebrows at her, obviously making the same connection she had: Charles had said something like this about

Jason Bell.

"What happened to Wornum?" she asked.

The cop did some more clicking and tapping. "Murder two, twenty-five to life. He died in prison three years ago."

"Can we go back to the report?"

She skimmed it over the cop's shoulder. Besides Ashley, there was one other witness, a next-door neighbor who said he'd heard the mother and boyfriend shouting at each other.

"What can you tell me about this guy, Albert Leone?" she said.

More tapping. "Seems to still live at the Sans Sucky. No record. Report says he was a dish washer."

Cynthia asked for a print out, and Jeff's GPS directed them to the Sans Sucky. It was indeed a dump, a row of separate brick buildings, one behind the other, with un-shuttered and in some cases duct-taped windows. Next to it was an even dumpier trailer park, the grounds cluttered with trash and faded plastic toys and discarded rusty appliances. One step up from homelessness, the Sans Sucky being the next step up. She wondered if Rachel's trailer park was this bad.

Leone was in the third building from the front, first level. She knocked, not hopeful he'd be home at this time of day, and knocked again, at which point the door opened on a diminutive, bleary-eyed man with tousled gray hair, dressed in a dingy white robe.

"Huh?" he said, looking up at her with something like amazement.

"Mr. Leone?" She showed him her badge. "We want to ask you about Alice Hunter's murder."

"Oh. I don't know nothing about that."

"You told the police you heard them shouting."

"Yeah. But that's all."

"We'd still like to talk to you. May we come in?"

"Okay, I guess," he said.

The place was tidier than Miriam Roxburys' but less pleasing in every other way. There was a saggy gray couch that looked as if it had been rescued from a curb, a little metal-legged table and couple of wooden chairs that might have had the same provenance, and an old TV on a stand, the shelf of which held an ancient VCR and a stack of cassettes, the top one showing naked bodies.

"I was asleep," Leone said, rubbing his eye. "I'm on a night clean-up crew."

"Sorry to wake you. The shouting you heard the evening Alice Hunter was killed, was that unusual?"

"No, ma'am. It was always like that."

"Had it ever led to violence before? You ever see Alice Hunter with a black eye or bruises?"

Leone shook his head.

"So did the murder surprise you?"

"I don't know. They was both drinkers."

"Her daughter Ashley said…" She was going to repeat the report's findings, as a preface to asking about Ashley's reaction to the murder, but Leone's reaction to the name was so nakedly, comically fearful, his mouth flying open and his eyes popping, that she stopped herself. Taking a chance, she said, "Be a good idea if you told us your side of the story."

He gazed at her hopelessly.

"You'll be doing yourself a favor," she said, still waiting to find out what she was talking about.

"It was all her idea," he said.

"How do you mean?"

"She come over with a camera and took the picture."

"What sort of a picture?" Cynthia said.

"She… put the camera on the table so she could be in it too."

"You didn't answer my question."

"She set on my lap."

"Is that all?"

"Uh, she unbuttoned her shirt."

Had Leone coerced Hunter somehow? But he'd said it was her idea, and he seemed too passive, and dim, to coerce anybody.

"You have sex with her?"

"No, ma'am. But she said if I didn't drive her, she'd show the picture to the police, and I'd go to jail."

"Drive her where?"

"To this school she was starting at."

"How long did you do that?"

"Till she moved away."

Three years, presumably. An hour round-trip, twice a day.

"Am I going to jail now?" Leone said.

"You're not under investigation, Mr. Leone." Returning to the question she'd intended to ask, she said, "Did you see Ashley the morning she discovered her mother's body?"

"No, ma'am. I saw the police, but I didn't see her."

"Did she ever say anything to you about it?"

"No, ma'am. Except I didn't need to drive her no more, 'cause she had her mother's car."

Was she gloating? Cynthia wondered. "How did she sound when she said it?"

Leone looked baffled. "I don't know. She just said it."

"Okay, Mr. Leone. Thanks."

"So I'm not going to jail?"

"No."

"I woulda drove her anyway, if she'd asked me," he said. "She was real pretty."

Chapter 17

"SLICK THE WAY YOU GOT Leone to open up," Jeff said, pulling out of the parking lot. He was driving so Cynthia could look at the police report. "Poor guy. He thought he was dealing with an honest cop."

"Those of us who can't ooze out the charm have to rely on other methods."

"I do not ooze. I empathize."

"Well, Mr. Lonely Hearts, how about Ashley Hunter—you empathize with her?"

"Nope. She gets a kick out of making people do things, even when there's nothing in it for her. No reason to give Miriam Roxbury a lifelong guilt trip."

"There's revenge," she said. "Punishing Miriam for having everything she didn't have."

"Okay. But blackmailing poor old dumb Leone—that must have been just for the fun of it. She had to know he'd do anything for her. She just preferred making him squirm."

"Fair point," Cynthia said. "Any thoughts on her mother's death?"

"Do I think she could have done it, you mean? Yeah, I do. She's got the personality for it. Plus she had opportunity. She just needed to wait until they'd both passed out. And motive: the car."

"Maybe revenge too. She apparently had reason to hate her mother, and strangulation is about as personal as murder gets."

"Okay. Now here's my question, or one of them. Before today, I was thinking of her as a possible informant in the Gates camp, paid by a full-fledged psychopath. But from what we heard, I like her as the psychopath, working for herself. But if that's true, where's the gain? When Gates quit the race, she was out of a job."

"I found out last night she's now Spencer's campaign manager."

"That's interesting. But he's not in the lead, is he?"

"No, but I think he's come up a bit."

"Still, why knock out the front runner to work for somebody who's iffy?"

"I don't know," she said. "But I agree she doesn't seem like anybody's stooge."

"And what about Bell, our bomb expert? How does he fit into all this?"

She shook her head. "His expertise is too big a coincidence to ignore, but I can't see him signing on to kill Kristen Gates."

"Hunter wouldn't need to tell him the girl would be there. She'd just need to talk him into blowing up the place."

"And how would she have gone about that?"

"She could've exploited his weaknesses," Jeff said, "like she did with Miriam and Leone. Drinker, PTSD. Right up her alley."

"Then what? Hunter instead of your terrorist vet plying him with liquor?"

"Right. It'd make him easy to kill—like her mother."

"So all we're missing," Cynthia said, "is a clear motive and solid evidence."

"Only that. Where do we go from here?"

"We could try to tie Hunter to Bell, but we'll need something more persuasive than the video you found linking her to Kristen. And to really work at it, we'll need Roger's backing—which I don't think we can get."

"Yeah. I'm beginning to lose faith in Roger," Jeff said. "His priorities are messed up. He puts groveling to Sampson ahead of groveling to you. If we want his support, we'd probably have to prove Hunter killed her mother, which I doubt we can do. The boyfriend confessed, sort of, and he's dead."

They lapsed into silence. Studying the report, she read that Hunter, upon discovering her mother's body, had run to a 7-11 to call the cops. She remembered passing the store on the way to Sans Sucky. It was a good mile from the complex. Why hadn't Hunter just gone next door to Leone's? Maybe she hadn't wanted the cops to connect them, since that might have led to Leone spilling the beans as he'd done today, putting her in a different light. It was another suggestive, and inconclusive, detail. Like Hunter saying, now she thought of it, that if Bell had been offered a campaign job, he hadn't been interested enough to pursue it with her. But he'd told his sister about it, which indicated he was interested and therefore had likely talked to Hunter.

She made a decision. "Here's what I think we should do," she said. "Write up what we know, and don't know, and what could still be explored, like seeing whether the unknown prints on Bell's car and the tire tracks beside it connect to Hunter. Then we give the report to the feds. If they find it persuasive enough, they'll have the resources to try and connect the dots."

"Hate to say it," Jeff said, "but I agree."

"Also, we can't send it through Roger or Sampson. They'll bury it. We'll have to go directly to the feds, and that carries a risk. Which is why I think I should do it alone. Since I've helped them with the case, I don't think Sampson will go after me. He hasn't so far."

Whether she was really safe, she didn't know. Sampson's warning to her may have evened the odds. But there was no point in both her and Jeff being in trouble, and she had a private motive he lacked. She could see Bertrand telling Reverend Brown about a second line of inquiry as a way to lessen the tensions, whatever was happening with the fake news crew. The report might help keep Rachel safe.

"Politics," Jeff said. "Why can't they just let us do our jobs?"

His rhetorical question, she took it, signaled his assent, so she let it be. For a few moments, she allowed herself to imagine an optimal outcome to the standoff, Brown in jail trying to convert his cellmates to the gospel of Brown, and Rachel back in the trailer park, having her baby in relative peace. Maybe then Sleeping Beauty would finally awaken.

Chapter 18

THE NUMBER OF PROTESTERS ON the roadside had doubled or maybe tripled since she was here last. There might be as many as a hundred. Another change had taken place too: most of the signs were about guns. One of them said, a little incoherently, "Second Amendment God-given Right!" Another: "Guns = Freedom." Neil Carson had succeeded in injecting his paranoia into the standoff.

She drove down to the barricade and spotted Archer and Bertrand. Sampson was with them, unfortunately, and so were two men she didn't recognize, one in a suit holding a folded umbrella and the other in jeans and a T-shirt, a big camera on his shoulder. The fake news crew, evidently.

Archer noticed her first. "Detective," he said.

Sampson, turning, scowled at her. He opened his mouth to speak, but she said quickly, "Sorry to interrupt, but I have some information that might be useful."

"We don't have time for your publicity-seeking, Westbrook," Sampson said, his face flushing beneath his prematurely white hair.

"What is it?" Archer asked.

"Someone on Gates's staff could be linked to the bombing. Circumstantial, but I thought you'd want to know."

She held out the folder with the report, and Archer took it.

"Thanks," he said. "I'll read it later. Little busy now."

"Yes, sir." She glanced at Sampson, who was still fuming.

"We set?" Bertrand said to the men.

They nodded, and he got out his phone and called a number. "Reverend Brown? Just wanted to let you know we're sending the news crew down." He put the phone away and looked at the overcast sky and then at the men. "Not raining yet. One good thing anyway. Okay. Good luck."

The agents started slowly down the drive. They moved in the double silence of the quiet day and the hush along the barricade. The colors of everything—the men's clothing, the dandelion-flecked grass, the gray stone of the house, the fitfully stirring flag—were deepened by the reduced light. When they reached the circular garden, the front door opened and everyone came out: first the three Defenders in full camouflage regalia with assault rifles slung across their vests, then Arnold, and last Brown and Rachel holding hands. Brown raised his free hand and smiled for the distant cameras. This was his idea, she knew. He was making sure he'd appear on the news before the promised airing of the interview.

Rachel, in the green trapeze dress she'd worn the first time Cynthia saw her, wasn't smiling with him, or showing any expression at all. She appeared to have retreated deep inside herself.

The fake newsmen stopped in front of the little group, and all of them stayed put.

"What's going on?" Archer said.

"Not sure," Bertrand said.

Face Paint, still identifiable as such, moved toward the men and patted them down. Carson said something to him, and he stuck his hand in their back pockets and pulled out their wallets. Carson took the wallets and began examining their contents.

"Why's he doing that?" Archer said. "They obviously aren't armed."

"They should be all right," Bertrand said. "They have CNN IDs."

Carson spoke to the agents, who responded. Shaking his head, he spoke again.

He's not buying it, Cynthia thought.

Suddenly Face Paint gave the one in the suit a little shove, and Tweedledee, admiring sidekick that he was, pointed his gun at the man. Then everything slowed as if she were watching a kabuki performance. With a look of alarm Carson reached for the gun barrel just as a bright red spray burst from Tweedledee's throat, followed by the belated crack of the sniper's rifle. Tweedledee dropped to his knees, and the two agents, casting umbrella and camera aside, took off for the trees on the right. Face Paint spun toward them with his rifle raised and was spun back again and then toppled by a hail of bullets. At this, Rachel, who'd been standing frozen beside Brown, jerked her hand free and staggered belly-heavy beyond the garden into the open.

"Get down!" Cynthia yelled to her.

Fully awake now, frantic, Rachel ran willy-nilly through the high grass. Behind her, Carson appeared above the garden wall, fired his gun, and disappeared.

Cynthia sprang onto the hood of the car that shielded her and slid across it to the lawn. "Down!" she yelled again.

Rachel turned at the sound of her voice and began stumbling uphill.

Cynthia ran toward her as Arnold ran after her, all three of them moving languorously as in a dream. The air filled with popping noises, and Arnold tottered and fell, and then in a kind of dance-like repetition, so did Rachel.

"No!" Cynthia shouted to no one, slipping, gaining her feet. Below her Rachel lay among the dandelions with her arms splayed and a great crimson stain spreading across the mound of her belly. A movement drew Cynthia's eye away from her: Carson rearing up again. He aimed his rifle at her, and in the adrenalin-stretched moment before he fired, she understood why he was going to shoot her. Believing the government would kill him, he wanted to take her with him as its only available representative. There was a strange comfort in knowing his motive wasn't personal and didn't negate his earlier civility.

A force hit her in the chest and thrust her backward. She had a moment of clarity in which she saw Carson collapse like a rag doll, and then she was on her back staring up at the gray sky.

Bertrand's bearded face appeared in her field of vision. Other faces appeared, Sampson's among them, gazing sternly down as if imposing final judgment. A strong hand pressed against her chest, inside which a vice was already squeezing her heart. The air resisted her efforts to suck it in. She closed her eyes and found herself in an immense dusky space like the sky. She wanted to tell Jack she was sorry, but he wasn't there. She told him anyway, blood gurgling in her throat.

Chapter 19

BITS AND PIECES AFTER THAT. A bumpy lift into the ambulance. A giant hand over her chest pulling the plunger of a hypodermic. Pain. Yellow hospital walls gliding by. Blue masks. Pain. Rain running silently down a window. Jack. A tube in her side. Pain.

And then a soft-voiced surgeon taking her through it. She'd been extremely lucky, he said. The bullet had broken a rib, penetrated her right lung and nicked her scapula on the way out, but despite its inner tumbling and fragmentation it had missed her heart, her spine, and the nearest artery.

She was in the hospital a week, although they had her up and walking as soon as possible to prevent pneumonia. Sally was there during the day fussing over her. Jack spent the evenings and the nights with her, sleeping on a fold-down chair that looked about as comfortable as a slab of rock.

"I'm all right," she said to him one evening.

"I know."

"You should go home to sleep. The nurses will look after me."

"I know."

But still he stayed.

Jeff came with Denise and Angela, and returned by himself for a few minutes every day, to Sally's delight. "He's such fun, isn't he?" she said after the first time.

"That's what all the girls think," Cynthia said. "The boys, not so much."

She also had some unexpected visitors. Her father drove up from Alabama with Alice Goff, both of whom she'd met investigating her mother's murder. They'd watched her get shot on the national news, something she had no intention of seeing herself. A while back, her father had taken her hint that Alice's old house was a good project for a handyman with leisure, and as he'd painted the porch and whatnot, the two of them had become friends.

"You need to stop this daring-do," said Alice, "and find yourself a more sensible occupation."

"I have a horse farm she can run," said Sally, who'd instantly hit it off with Alice.

Her father, staying out of it, examined the stack of books Jack had brought from her night table. "Updike," he said. "The man could write. How's this one?" He held up *Middlemarch*.

"Great," Cynthia said. "My third go around with it. You can take it if you want."

"No, no, I can get my own copy."

"You can borrow mine," Alice said. "I have her other novels, too, if you like that one."

She hadn't seen Alice and her father together before, and if she hadn't known better, she might have mistaken them for mother and son, their height discrepancy notwithstanding: Alice came in somewhere under five feet, and her father was six-three or four. They were another Mutt and Jeff team like her and Jeff, though an even more conspicuous one. But they both had a sort of outsider aura that linked them, Alice with her wild white hair and green eyeshade, her father with his long-haired hippie insouciance and the red squid tattoo on his forearm. More important, they had an ease with each other that seemed familial. Alice was childless and Cynthia's father had been alienated from his parents, so it made her happy to see them together—an otherwise elusive feeling since the shooting.

Mid-week she received a collect call from Mike Fallon. "Welcome to the club," he said. "At least you lived to tell the tale."

"I don't think I'll be telling it. Not my finest moment."

"Saw it on the news. You were trying to save that girl. What happened to her wasn't your fault."

But it was my fault, she thought. *If I'd done nothing, she might still be alive. Arnold might have grabbed her near the garden and pulled her down.*

"So how are you feeling?" she said.

"Better than you at the moment, I imagine. Been re-reading the poems in that book you gave me. Every time I do, I get something a little different out of them."

"The nature of poems."

"There's another one by Yeats I like, about going away to an island and planting beans."

"The Lake Isle of Innisfree."

"Right. Maybe you should plant some beans of your own and sit around and watch them grow."

"Guess I'll have to do something like that for a few weeks anyway. Then I'm coming to see you."

"Don't bother about me," he said. "Just focus on getting better. Oh, I told Decker I was going to call, and he said to send you his regards."

Decker, the Maryland cop who'd taken Fallon into custody, had become his friend too, though their relationship was likely less fraught than hers was with him.

"He still on the job?" she said.

"Yep. He also said to tell you he's waiting for a call—whatever that means."

"Old joke of his. Phone sex."

"Oh." Fallon sounded embarrassed, as if her sexual nature weren't something he cared to think about.

Later on the same day she received a call from Roger, who sounded stressed even as he acknowledged her thanks for the flowers he'd sent. "Look," he said, his voice quavering, "I know it isn't the best time, but I need to tell you that as of today you're suspended—with pay. The sheriff's ordered an investigation of your actions in the shooting incident."

As soon as she heard this, she knew what would happen. Sampson would see to it she was fired. And if she were in his shoes, she might do the same thing.

Two weeks after her release from the hospital, she appeared before the board of inquiry and answered their questions about what she'd done and why. The chair, a sour-faced man with beetling eyebrows, addressed her at the end. "As I see it," he said, "you were there without the sheriff's permission, in fact against his explicit instructions, and your actions not only contributed to Ms. Dudley's death but also endangered your fellow officers who, distracted by you, might have become targets." A few days later the board formalized these points in its report, and it was all the ammunition Sampson needed.

Roger called again to give her the news. After reading from the letter of termination she'd yet to receive, he signed off with a woeful "Sorry." Two hours later Jeff showed up at the house.

"You hear from Roger?" he said.

She nodded.

"Well, this just sucks. You should fight it."

"I don't see how."

His silence indicated he didn't either. She asked him if he had any new pictures of Angela, and as he showed them to her, she realized they were consoling each other over the end of their partnership. It was a loss she hadn't taken into account until now.

When he put his phone away, he said with forced casualness, "Okay, pard, gotta go."

They stood and hugged, requiring her to stoop so his head would be level with hers.

"Let's not do that again," he said.

"Okay."

At the door, he said, "Roger was too chickenshit to fire you in person, but I'll give him this. Word is he persuaded Sampson to suspend you with pay, and to put off the inquiry long enough for the county to cover your hospital bills."

She was grateful for Roger's intervention; it humanized the process and even humanized Sampson a bit for listening to Roger. But she was already resigned to her fate. This didn't mean, however, she was ready to move on. Whenever her thoughts turned to the future, a great blank loomed in her mind. She felt as if she'd died in the shootout and was haunting her former life. The analogy, she knew, was both self-pitying and inexact. She wasn't invisible to the people who cared about her. Jack had taken her out on Belmont Bay in his motorboat, and during a long and soothing excursion, the water calm and the day bright and cool, he'd said without preamble, and with uncharacteristic intensity, "The only ones to blame are the men in that house. You were a victim too, and that's all you were." But she'd lost her calling, and she couldn't shake the feeling she deserved it. At random moments she'd flash back to Rachel stumbling toward her, or Neil Carson aiming his rifle at her; and the two memories came to signify her crime and her punishment.

She took refuge in reading and especially in working at the farm. She had lingering and sometimes compelling pain in her chest and back, and her right arm still wouldn't go any higher than her shoulder, but she could do the lighter tasks or anyway play at being useful. The farm, with its orange-tinged rolling meadows and distant blue mountains, its cloud-piled canopy and breezes and silences, was her Lake Isle of Innisfree. Here, as Yeats said, peace came dropping slow. Her favorite job was grooming the horses. When she was with them, running her hand over their coarse-haired skin, inhaling their pleasantly earthy smell, and looking into their beautiful dark eyes, she felt in contact with a state of being that was simpler and more immediate than her own, one that was free of both the past and the future.

Meanwhile, humanity proceeded according to its nature. She didn't seek information about the aftermath of the shootout, but it came to her as if by osmosis. Someone would say something, or she'd hear a report on the car radio. In this way she learned that Brown, the only survivor from the house, was no longer a suspect in the bombing, and that the charges against him arising from the standoff had been dropped, his lawyer having successfully portrayed him as Arnold's de facto hostage. Also, the publicity had turned him into a significant figure in the pro-life movement. Instead of protesting outside clinics, he now spoke at rallies and on religious TV and radio. Rachel figured in his remarks as a martyr to the cause and an exemplar to women considering abortion. And since a Marshal's bullet had killed her, she lived on as well in reports about her mother's lawsuit against the government. Nor was she the only martyr among the shootout dead. Carson, his comrades in arms, and Arnold had all been accorded that status by the militia movement, which had posted their pictures and the video of their deaths on its websites. Inspired by their sacrifice, an Ohio militia had briefly prevented police from arresting one of its own for spousal abuse.

As for Ashley Hunter, no word had reached Cynthia's ears. The candidate she'd worked for after Gates dropped out, the obnoxious Sam Spencer, had lost the Republican nomination to George Allen in June, but Cynthia didn't have any more direct knowledge of her than that. She also didn't know if the FBI had followed up on her report about Hunter and Bell. But given her fall from grace and, according to Jack, the somewhat less steep fall of Archer, who'd been removed from the case, she doubted it.

The lack of information added to her surprise when Jeff told her his investigation of Hunter was getting nowhere. They were having lunch, as they'd been doing every week or so since her firing, and she looked around the restaurant for other sheriff's personnel.

"You need to stop," she said.

"I owe it to you. I should've gone with you that morning."

She shook her head. "We decided it was too risky for you, and it still is."

"I'm being careful."

"All it takes is one slip. You know how Sampson feels. He gets wind of what you're up to and he'll treat you as a substitute for me."

"That's not my only reason," Jeff said. "If we're right about Hunter, I'm betting she'll kill again."

"*If* we're right. You just said you were getting nowhere."

"True," he admitted. "People I've talked to think she's the cat's meow."

"So maybe we were wrong about her."

Before they parted, she extracted from him a promise to give it up. And in dissuading him, she mostly dissuaded herself from believing in Hunter's guilt. What did they have on her, after all? She'd blackmailed a man who would have done her bidding anyway, which reduced her coercion to a kind of sport, and she'd played head games with a pliable girl, though without hurting the family dog, which made her less guilty in a certain sense than Luna's captors. Clearly she wasn't a nice person, but it was a leap from that to the presumption of murder.

As a result of this train of thought, Cynthia sank even deeper into self-recrimination. The mistakes she'd made, getting Rachel killed and wrecking her career, were due to a hunch she'd had about the bombing, nothing more.

Chapter 20

THE STARKNESS OF THIS REALIZATION was dispiriting, but it was also freeing. So far as her job was concerned, the past appeared to her as a charred landscape, like Hemingway's burned over country in *Big, Two-Hearted River*, and there was nothing to be done but fish somewhere else. Where, exactly, she balked at deciding, but she felt now the inevitability of choosing a path.

Late one afternoon relaxing with Sally, the two of them drinking sweet tea in the den, she heard herself ask, "What do you think I should do?"

"What do you want to do, honey?" Sally said.

"I don't know. The only thing that comes to mind is teach English."

"You said once you'd probably have been a teacher if you hadn't joined the sheriff's."

"I remember. What I meant was, there's not much else an English major can do."

"Well, why don't you talk to one of your old professors? Maybe they can help you make up your mind, one way or the other."

And so, after more hesitation, she took Sally's advice and called Ruth Ayers, the head of the English department at Mary Weaver College. She'd not only taken a class from Dr. Ayers but also interviewed her about the disappearance of Fallon's niece, another English teacher at the college. They arranged to meet the next morning, and when Cynthia entered Allen Hall shortly before nine and started up the broad marble staircase, she felt like a kid going to a teacher/student conference.

The marble steps gave way to narrow flights of creaking wood that took her to the English aerie on the third floor. Dr. Ayers' office was reached through the department office, and when she stepped inside the glassed room, the secretary, who was new to her, asked if she could help.

"I know where I'm going," Cynthia said, realizing the irony as she said it. "Here to see Dr. Ayers."

Dr. Ayers answered her knock and invited her to sit in one of the chairs facing each other on a little corded rug. A stout, gray-haired woman with green eyes and latte-colored skin, she had a serious, though not self-important, manner. "As I mentioned on the phone," she said, "I'm aware of recent events. How are you?"

"All right. Almost back to normal."

"But you're... considering a new direction."

"Yes. Though not by choice."

"Ah." Instead of asking for details, Dr. Ayers merely looked at her.

"I noticed there's a new secretary," Cynthia said. "What happened to Laura?"

"She's working in the private sector now."

"Why did she leave? Did it have anything to do with Alicia Bradford's death?"

"That may have been part of it, yes."

"And the poet—is he still here?"

"Walter Lewis? He's still with us, though he's in England at the moment, in Wordsworth country."

"His wife and kids go with him?"

"No. Sadly, she moved back to where she was from—Iowa, I believe—taking the children with her." Dr. Ayers smiled and folded her hands in her lap. "So, the new direction for you may be school."

Unable to put it off any longer, Cynthia said, "What do you think of the idea?"

"After you called, I reviewed your record, which confirmed my memory of you as a superior student. I'm sure you'd have no trouble, academically speaking."

She noted the qualification. "How about non-academically speaking?"

"I regard you as quite young, of course," Dr. Ayers said, "but your fellow students will see you from their somewhat intolerant perspective."

"So I shouldn't count on getting asked out to movie night at the student union."

Dr. Ayers smiled again. "You might feel a little isolated. Not a major obstacle, but something to be prepared for. Also, if you want to teach English above the public-school level, you'll need at least a Master's, and for a university position, a doctorate."

"You think I'm capable of that—getting a higher degree, I mean?"

"I'm certain of it. And if you choose to come back to us, I'll do everything in my power to smooth the way."

Driving home from North Hill, Cynthia tried to imagine herself as both a student and a teacher. The first was easy to do since she'd been one. She'd enjoyed attending lectures and doing the work, and still would, she thought, even if her classmates looked at her askance. The second was not so easy. What would it entail? Lecturing. Preparing lectures. Grading papers. Being in one place all day. The lack of mobility struck her as particularly off-putting. But she was a reader, and took pleasure in introducing people to books. That seemed a good start. Maybe the idea of teaching would grow on her.

When she reached Calvary, she turned south on impulse and headed toward the farm. Sally would be supportive of anything she wanted to do, and although that shouldn't help her make up her mind, she felt in need of positive reinforcement. Sally's green pickup wasn't parked out front, as it usually was this time of day, but it could be in the garage. She let herself in and found Maria in the den watching a soap.

"She out running errands," Maria said, "I jus made some apple empanadas. I get you some."

Cynthia declined the offer, to no avail. "Mr. Jack was feeding you good," Maria said. "But now you too eskinny again." She disappeared into the kitchen.

Trying to ignore the soap voices ("I'm sorry, Seth, but I've fallen in love with Eli."), she went over to the picture window. The hilltop cemetery's low fence stood out against the sky, revealing the shape of a leafy weed sprouting above it. After she'd eaten one of Maria's empanadas and begged off the other two on the plate, though agreeing to take them with her, she fetched the short-handled shovel from the mud room and walked up to the cemetery.

The little metal gate creaked as she opened it, but this was the only sound. Silence reigned here. If Juan and Reggie were banging about in the stables, or the horses scattered below were nickering or blowing, she couldn't hear it. Overhead, a hawk soared on a high and soundless wind. She pulled at the tall weed, and when it broke off near the ground, as she'd anticipated, she picked up the shovel. Pushing the blade into the soil, she thought how agreeable it was to perform a simple physical task in such a beautiful setting. Maybe she should fulfill Sally's wish and take over the management of the farm. She'd resisted partly because the work wasn't challenging enough—the very thing she now liked about it—but mainly because it would set in motion the succession that Sally desired and that presaged her death.

From the corner of her eye, she glimpsed a figure coming up the hill. She assumed it was Sally, home from her errands; but when she turned and looked, she saw a blond-haired woman dressed in a ruffled blouse, tight jeans, and tall boots. She didn't recognize her, and then she did. It was Ashley Hunter.

Chapter 21

CYNTHIA TIGHTENED HER HOLD ON the shovel handle. Her sense of danger, she felt, was irrational. Nothing in Hunter's manner or appearance gave cause for alarm. Nevertheless, she regretted the limited use of her arm. If she had to defend herself, she wouldn't be able to raise the shovel high enough to take a two-handed swing at Hunter's skull.

Hunter, climbing, met her stare with a slight smile. When she reached the cemetery, she put her hand on the gate and said, "May I?"

"What are you doing here?" Cynthia said.

"I wanted to see you, and since you weren't home, I thought you might be at your friend Sally's. The housekeeper told me you were up here."

"How would you know about Sally and this place?"

"I've taken an interest in you, Cynthia," Hunter said, "just as you and your partner once did in me. I understand he kept asking about me after you were fired, but now he seems to have stopped. Maybe fatherhood has distracted him."

Whatever doubts she may have had about Hunter's guilt, the implied threats in this little speech completely erased.

"Has he stopped?" Hunter said.

For Jeff's sake, she told the truth: "Yes."

"That's good." Hunter pushed on the gate. "May I?" she said again.

Cynthia nodded.

Stepping inside, Hunter glanced at the grave stones. "Who are these people?"

"The family who once lived here."

"What about this one?" She pointed to Bill's marker. "He's more recent than the others. Friend of yours?"

"Yes."

"So that's why you're up here. I wondered." Hunter shaded her eyes with her hand and looked toward the mountains. "The view's nice, too. Though seeing it from a cemetery detracts a little, don't you think? I've never been one for memento mori, the skull on the table, that sort of thing. Life is for the living, I say."

When Cynthia didn't respond, Hunter said, "You know, that time you came to the campaign office, I instantly felt a connection to you. And when I Googled you, I understood why. We're both the children of single mothers—bastards, not to put too fine a point on it. And we've both had, let's say, problematic childhoods. You were orphaned at an early age, and I was always an orphan, in a sense. Did you feel the same thing about me?"

"No."

"No? Well, I guess it wouldn't have mattered if you had, since you apparently decided I was a suspect. Though suspected of what, I can't imagine."

Hunter's visit was also a fishing expedition, Cynthia realized. She could tell her nothing or see where things went. "The murder," she said, "of Kristen Gates, Dr. Beatty, Officer Steve Williams,

Jason Bell, and your mother." And indirectly, she thought, of the people in the house. Rachel. Though Rachel's death was a shared responsibility, something they did have in common.

Hunter laughed. "Well, I admit to hating my mother. That qualifies as a motive, I suppose. But what would be my reason for killing those other people?"

"Bell because he blew up the clinic for you."

"Why would I want it blown up?"

"To kill Kristen," Cynthia said, "though I doubt Bell knew she'd be there."

"And why would I want to do that?"

"You tell me."

Hunter shook her head. "No. You tell me. You're the accuser. You're the one who's gone around asking questions about me, tarnishing my reputation."

Cynthia, having nothing to say, remained silent.

"You don't have a theory, do you?" Hunter said. "Well, I'm not a detective, or a former detective, but I can imagine some possibilities. How about this? I signed on with Gates because he had the best chance of being nominated. He was a war hero and a nice man, so the base liked him well enough, even if he was a little soft on certain issues. And then Sam Spencer entered the race. He was young and good looking and a real fire breather on the stump. Most important, he didn't have a moderate bone in his body. He was perfect for the base. I could see it in the crowds at his rallies—their enthusiasm, their anger. He was the future, not Gates. So I decided to switch teams. But it was a tricky thing to do without hurting my career, and while I was trying to think of a way, Kristen, who might have misinterpreted my friendliness, confided she was pregnant and asked for my help. She knew the news of her abortion wouldn't be good for her father. Of course, that was exactly the outcome I desired. So I arranged things for her, planning to tip the media off. Then Bell appeared, and I saw a way to improve my plan."

She stopped and met Cynthia's gaze. "What do you think? Full of holes or sea worthy?"

Listening to this, Cynthia had experienced a strong physical revulsion, as if she'd inhaled a whiff of something vile. But at the same time, she'd been conscious of a disturbing feeling of complicity. She'd given Hunter permission to come in, as it were, and allowed her to flirt and gloat, and she'd done it not out of any hope of putting her away—there was little chance of that, under the circumstances—but out of the desire to know. Out of curiosity.

In as calm a voice as she could manage, she said, "How would killing Kristen be an improvement?"

"Oh, extra insurance, I would think. No one to tell the tale and make future employers wary of me."

"Why would the doctor, who had no reason to protect a conservative politician, moderate or not, be willing to perform the abortion in secret?"

Hunter shrugged. "Money? Or maybe a promise that Gates would oppose the defunding of the clinics. I like the second idea. It preserves the doctor's dignity."

But not his life. "And Bell? How did you persuade him to blow up the clinic? I doubt money would have done it."

"How did I persuade him *theoretically*," Hunter reminded her. "Well, from what I've read, he was a troubled veteran who admired the General. Possibly he could have been led to believe the bombing would help Gates—give him an opportunity to show the decent man he is, condemning the destruction as a violation of all that binds us together, whatever our views on abortion."

"Doesn't sound like an easy sell," Cynthia said.

"Depends on the seller. And the means of persuasion."

"You saying you slept with him?"

"I'm not talking about myself at all. I'm just fleshing out your fantasy of me."

"The rumor about Gates and his daughter," Cynthia said, refusing to go along with the charade. "My guess is you started it, but I don't see how it could have helped you. Gates had already dropped out by then."

Hunter smiled. "My job involves following polls, so I may have noticed a development you didn't. Spencer's numbers went down after his comment on Kristen's death, but they went up again when the father of the baby came forward, and turned out to be black."

It was hard to take in—impossible, really. On top of Kristen's murder, Hunter had subjected her parents to the additional agony of the rumor, just to gain a few points in the polls. "But Spencer didn't get the nomination," Cynthia said. "So it was all for nothing."

"I wouldn't say that. Consider the big picture. He got himself noticed, on the national level too. And he'll run again. Plans are already in the works."

Her hazel eyes bright with interest in the subject, Hunter could have been opining on a Sunday morning news show. What would it be like to be her? Cynthia wondered. To feel neither love nor remorse. To count murder privately among your triumphs. Maybe at times it was lonely, and that was one reason she was here. "I don't suppose you bothered," she said, "to justify the carnage to yourself."

"Not my carnage to justify," Hunter said. "But it's always a matter of perspective, isn't it? While we're having our little chat, doctors are killing innocents in the womb, and American drones are killing innocents in the Middle East. This country was built on the corpses of Indians and the bloody backs of slaves. The truth is, everyone is expendable for the right reasons—your own reasons."

"If you really believe that, how did you choose a side?"

Hunter stuck her finger into the air. "Like this."

Hit her in the knees, Cynthia thought, *and when she's down, the head, and bury her here.*

Something of this desire must have revealed itself in her face or posture, for Hunter, with a startled look, took a backward step.

"Get out," Cynthia said.

Recovering quickly, perhaps because she saw the danger was past, the murderous urge channeled into words, Hunter said, "One other thing. Maybe Bell's death was just what it seemed. Your fantasy version of me might have learned about it from the news, like everybody else, and been saved some trouble. I know you're literary—I read it in a story about you. You'll appreciate, then, just as I have, Edmund's line from *Lear: Now gods, stand up for bastards.* Take care, Cynthia."

Hunter let herself out and walked at an easy pace down the hillside. Cynthia, gripping the shovel, her heart hammering in her throat, watched her go.

Chapter 22

SHE WAITED UNTIL HUNTER'S CAR—a discreet gray Camry, which might have followed her without her noticing—appeared on the drive going toward the road. Then she went back down to the house.

Maria, sitting in front of the TV again, said, "You have a nice talk with your friend?"

"Yes."

"You okay, Miss Cynthia? You look kinda pale."

"Just not up to full speed yet. Tell Sally I'm sorry I missed her."

"You no gonna wait for her?"

"No, I've got somewhere else to be." If she stayed, Sally would also see there was something wrong and question her about it.

As she headed toward the door, Maria called after her, "Wait, you forgot your empanadas!"

Maria hurried into the kitchen and came back carrying a plastic bag with at least six empanadas in it. "For Mr. Jack too," she said. "I know how much he like them."

Cynthia drove in the direction of home, thinking that Ashley Hunter's car might be somewhere ahead of her. It occurred to her, too, that Jeff had been right about Hunter being the killer rather than the killer's stooge, and about her exploiting Bell's vulnerability. But she could never tell him. He'd dive back into the case, and this time he might get caught and fired. There was also no point in telling Roger and Sampson. Sampson wouldn't believe her, and Roger, whatever he believed, wouldn't go against Sampson. They'd never seek a warrant to examine Hunter's tires and take her finger prints. That left the FBI, and with Archer off the case, she doubted she could convince them to do anything—even if Jack, when she told him, could get her an audience with Archer's replacement. It'd still be the word of a disgraced county employee against a hotshot, Harvard-educated politico. She also doubted that the evidence at the scene of Bell's death would implicate Hunter. That would appear to be the point of Hunter's comment about Bell— she hadn't needed to do anything, to touch anything. The gods had stood up for her. Cynthia remembered Jack's speculation that Bell might have accidentally come upon the road into the wood. Hunter, though no doubt intending to murder him, may not have known where he was.

Approaching the road to her house, Cynthia suddenly didn't feel like waiting around for Jack to arrive. She needed to be doing something. She remembered her promise to Mike Fallon that she'd see him soon. Today, she knew, was a visitors' day at the prison, and if she just kept going, she'd arrive there before visiting hours ended.

❀ ❀ ❀

When Mike showed up on the other side of the glass, she was shocked at his appearance. Above the scruffy gray beard, his cheeks were hollow, and his sunken eyes had a sickly glitter.

"How are you?" she said.

He shrugged. "I've felt better. How about you? Healing up okay?"

"I'm coming along."

"You found anything to do with yourself?"

"Thinking about going back to school."

"Sounds like a plan," he said.

"Yeah."

"You don't seem too happy about it."

"Well, my feelings are mixed. But it isn't that. It's... I saw someone today, before I came here." And then it just spilled out of her, everything: her suspicions about Ashley Hunter, what she and Jeff had discovered, the dead ends, the reason she'd gone to the standoff, and Hunter showing up today and smugly confessing, under the veil of theorizing, to murder.

As he listened, Fallon seemed to gain strength. He sat up straighter, his eyes sharpened with interest. "No way to get at her, then?" he said.

"Not that I see."

He gave her his hard cop's stare. "You aren't thinking of doing anything stupid, are you?"

"No. But if she comes after Sally or someone else because of me..."

"Why would she? She's free and clear. You need to forget about her and get on with your life."

"Not so easy to do."

"Better than driving yourself crazy. Or ending up in a place like this."

The voice on the phone told them time was nearly up.

"Forget her," Fallon repeated.

"I'll see you in a few days, Mike."

"Look, long as you're here, I just wanna say your visits have meant a lot. The books too."

He put his hand on the greasy glass, something he'd never done before. She did the same, aligning her hand with his.

"Big hand," he said.

"Comes with the territory."

"Take care, Cynthia."

Thinking those had been Hunter's last words too, she said, "And you."

He got up slowly and moved toward the exit on his side of the booths.

❖ ❖ ❖

She made it home before Jack did. Still agitated, she poured herself a glass of wine and took it outside to the little backyard. Sitting in the wooden swing left by a previous occupant, she gazed at the woods behind the wire fence. When she first saw them, their nearness to the house had reminded her of the woods behind her childhood home, in which she'd hidden from her mother's killer and then gotten lost and almost died. But those trees had also been part of her life before her mother's death, her happy life. You couldn't separate the good memories from the bad; if you wanted the one, you had to accept the other. That was something she'd finally learned after years of suppressing both.

Jack, when he first saw the house, had said it looked like his childhood home, and this had given her another reason to like it. Living in it, she felt as if she were communing a bit with the Jack she'd never known, the scrawny kid in the photos she'd seen, the geeky introvert who didn't wish to be anything else. The house was a white clapboard shoebox with a central concrete stoop—six steps to the door—flanked by double windows with green-and-white striped canvas awnings. The interior, only a thousand square feet over a basement, consisted of two bedrooms, a cramped, plaid-wallpapered bath, a narrow kitchen with ancient appliances, a den and a dining room, and a so-called enclosed back porch that was hardly more than a walk-through closet. She could imagine

Jack playing with his two brothers in a house like this, or more likely, finding a quiet corner and disappearing into books as she'd done too.

Besides conjuring the past, the place had fit their basic criteria. They'd wanted a somewhat rural setting and a modest rent (Jack was putting his daughter through Stanford). They'd talked about re-painting the interior, including the chipped, old-fashioned radiators in most of the rooms, and improving the little yard with shrubbery and flowers. But other things had intervened. So it wasn't quite home yet. And the same might be said of their relationship. They were still creating a life together, while each of them simultaneously pursued a new line of work, Jack by choice and she by necessity. It was a complicated situation. It was also a good reason to take Mike Fallon's advice and forget Ashley Hunter. Focus on making this work. One way to do it, she thought, was to say nothing to Jack about Hunter. The fact she hadn't mentioned her so far would help. In the rush of events leading up to the shootout, there hadn't been time to bring her up, and afterward, she hadn't felt like it, not until today.

She tried to imagine a life free of Hunter. A life with Jack and Sally, Hunter fading from it like a dissolving cloud: the vapor subdividing, becoming wisps, then vanishing. As if in mockery of this hope, a huge crow flapped down into the grass and, cocking its head in her direction, squawked loudly. It might as well have said, "Nevermore."

Chapter 23

SHE DIDN'T SEE FALLON AGAIN. Twelve days after her visit, Decker, his Maryland cop friend, called her to say he'd died. "He was on his way out," he said, "but it was still quicker than I expected. Cell mate found him in his bunk. Think he must've wanted it."

"That's what he told me," she said.

"Guy called me, a lawyer, said he was executor of the estate and had some discretionary funds to pay for a funeral, if I wanted to arrange it. So I found out where Mike's family is buried in Baltimore. Turns out the niece is there too, and since all the nearby space was taken, I decided to put his ashes in her plot. Seemed like the right thing to do, even if the Bradford side of the family might object—but I didn't tell 'em. They'll never know the difference, up there in Boston. This Saturday morning at ten, if you're interested."

Jack, knowing of her feelings for Fallon, and the complexity of those feelings, insisted on going with her. She drove them there in an hour and half, taking the northern route, and they met Decker outside the caretaker's office. He was with another man whom he introduced as Bill Grayson, Fallon's lawyer. Grayson was a storklike personage with a big Adam's apple and a somewhat elusive air. When she asked him if he'd known Fallon long, he said, "Not really, no." His dark suit, which looked as cheap as Decker's blue one, suggested he hadn't reached the heights of his profession.

Round face grinning beneath a straw pork pie, Decker gave Jack the once over. "So you're the lucky man," he said.

"I am," said Jack.

"Good you know it." He gave his pants a hitch over his pot belly. "Guess we might as well get this show on the road."

He went in and summoned the caretaker, an elderly man who seemed grateful for the company, and they all caravanned behind the caretaker to the burial plot. Grayson emerged from his car with a small black umbrella under one arm and a black plastic box in his hands.

"Is that it?" Decker said, staring at the box.

"It's what comes with the cremation," Grayson said. "Anything else is extra, but they assured me it's quite sturdy."

"Well, it'll probably outlast wood and metal," Decker said.

They walked through several rows of graves, some with withered or artificial flowers, to Alicia Bradford's resting place. It had an oversized headstone with a bas-relief of a girl reading a book, appropriate for a specialist in children's literature. The Bradfords must have ordered it, Cynthia thought. The plot had been prepared in advance, though not much had been involved. At its center was a small hole with a patch of artificial turf to one side.

"When the marker comes in," the caretaker said, "we'll put it right under the headstone."

Grayson handed him the box, and he bent down and placed it on the patch of fake grass. This was all the ceremony Fallon was going to get, it seemed.

"Mike ought to like it here," Decker said, glancing at the nearby graves, "except for his brother-in-law. Kind of a funny story he told me about him. Before the car accident that killed him and his wife and the other daughter, the guy had asked for a divorce. Both sides of the family knew it, but not the niece, so for her sake they buried her folks side by side. Only reason they're together."

The day was hot, and the grave, like most of those in the wide old cemetery, lay exposed to the sun. She'd worn a wool skirt because it was black, a mistake; she could already feel sweat trickling down her inner thighs. Everyone else was feeling the heat too, except maybe Jack, who had a Zen-like indifference to weather. The underarms of Decker's coat were dark with perspiration, and Grayson, after offering his umbrella to her and Jack, opened it over his bald pate.

"Well," Decker said, "I don't have a speech, but here goes. Uh, Mike had his good points. He was a good cop, I understand. I called his old precinct to see if anybody wanted to come, but the ones who'd known him had either moved away or kicked the bucket. Anyway, he and I had some interesting talks in the joint. Cop stories, mostly. Too bad we couldn't have shot the breeze over a beer." He paused. "Guess that's it for me. Cynthia, you wanna say anything?"

Not having planned on it, she took a moment, and then stitched together from memory a few lines of "The Lake Isle of Innisfree":

I will arise and go now, and go to Innisfree
And I shall have some peace there, for peace comes dropping slow
There midnight's all a glimmer, and noon a purple glow.

"That beats me," Decker said. "We might as well plant him."

"No need to stay," the caretaker said. "We'll do the rest."

"Okay, then," Decker said.

They walked back to their cars.

"Thought we might get some coffee or something," Decker said, "but I don't know any greasy spoons around here. Grayson, you know a place?"

"No, sorry," Grayson said, folding his umbrella. "And pardon me, but I have another engagement."

"Another funeral?"

"A wedding, actually. My wife's cousin."

He then folded himself into his small car and pulled away.

Jack shook hands with Decker and climbed into the passenger seat of her car. Before she got in too, Decker said, "Nothing wrong with that voice of yours. How's the rest of you?"

"Good."

"They handed you a shit deal."

"Well, I appreciate the sentiment."

"Gimme a call sometime, so we can exchange pleasantries."

"In your dreams."

He laughed. "Like everything else."

❖ ❖ ❖

The conversation with Ashley Hunter in the farm's little cemetery had decided her against going to work for Sally; the encounter had left a stain on the place. And since she neither trusted herself to do police work nor believed any local force would hire her after so public a failure, that reduced her options to school. Over the next couple of weeks, she tried to focus on becoming a student again. She selected the English courses of most interest to her from the college's online catalog, found out what she could about the texts for them, and ordered the books.

She also went to a dress shop for younger women, thinking the right clothes might help her blend in. But after she'd squeezed into several pairs of circulation-cutting jeans and tried on a few short, brightly colored dresses and some black leggings that made her look, with her long legs, as if she were part grasshopper, she decided to stick with her usual slacks and blouses. Besides, the face that stared back at her from the dressing room mirror would never pass for twenty, and even if it had retained the smooth plumpness of youth, that wouldn't change anything: age wasn't just physical. She bought the leggings since she'd taken them out of the package, knowing they'd end up in the bottom of a drawer.

One morning after Jack had left for work, as she was reading the Post with her third cup of coffee, before deciding which text to explore, she came across a brief article about a murder in Alexandria, a woman shot to death in her apartment. The victim, age 32, was named Ashley Hunter.

She called Jeff. He hadn't seen the story, so she read it to him.

"Wow," he said. "That must be our Ashley."

"Could you make sure, and find out what you can about it?"

An hour later he called back. "Our Ashley, all right. Cops there think it was a burglary gone bad. Bedroom ransacked, jewelry box empty. They figure she came home and surprised the intruder, who shot her. But there's one problem with this scenario: she was shot in the head at close range."

"More execution style than heat of the moment."

"Right. I pointed this out to the cop in charge of the investigation, but he didn't appreciate my input."

"Maybe it's the way you pointed it out."

"Well, I may have questioned his powers of perception. You think this has anything to do with the bombing?"

"I don't know. But it's another big coincidence."

When she hung up she called Decker.

Answering on the first ring, he said, "I've worn you down."

"Not yet. But I'd like to listen to *you* talk—about Mike Fallon's lawyer."

"Grayson? He's sort of a bottom feeder from what I could tell. The kind that hangs around prisons looking for work. Not mobbed up or anything. Mike probably heard about him from another con."

"Could you ask him what happened to Mike's estate?"

"Sure. But why?"

She told him everything.

"Okay," he said. "Gimme a day or two."

He called back the following day. "Here's the story," he said. "Originally, any remainder after the state collected was supposed to go to a scholarship in his niece's name, at the college where she taught, except for a small percentage to the prison library. Then just a few days before he died—after you saw him—he asked Grayson to send the library share plus most of the other to a Baltimore cop friend who'd fallen on hard times. Ten grand in cash. Which sounded hinky to me, especially since I couldn't scout up any cop friends for the burial. And when I checked on this guy, I found out he'd fallen on hard times all right—twenty years ago, killed making an arrest. The address Grayson sent the money to was a P.O. box in the cop's name. There might be surveillance footage of whoever rented it, but it'll likely show somebody in a hood or a hat, head down. But I'll stay with it. If this is what it looks like, Mike might have gotten in touch with the renter through another con."

"You think Grayson knows more than he's saying?" she asked.

"I think he prefers ignorance. But even if he does know something, the cop's name on the P.O. box gives him plenty of cover." Decker let out a mirthless laugh. "Looks like you were a late addition to Mike's will."

Chapter 24

DECKER'S IRONIC CRACK HAD ANOTHER level of which only she was aware. She'd rejected Fallon's money because of his bloody deed, but she'd become his beneficiary through another bloody deed. There was more here too, but she skittered away from thinking about it. Then one morning starting out for Sally's she changed direction and, after some aimless driving through the countryside, headed toward the place where Bell's body had been discovered. Why she was going there, she wasn't sure, but it felt like something she needed to do.

The trees on either side of the dead-end road now had their full summer foliage, dark green and abundant, and as she drove slowly between them, their leafy shadows crawled across the windshield. No dirty Mustang this time, or empty-eyed Jason Bell. But there was a resonance, at least for her. She parked where he had parked to work himself up to putting a bullet through his head. He'd done it, apparently, out of remorse for the bombing deaths. Remembering the tidy air of his motel room, the liquor bottles lined up against the wall, she guessed he would have staked out the clinic for several nights running to make sure no one was around. So at the end he might have been tortured by the thought that if he'd lingered there on the fatal night, he would've seen the doctor's car go around back and had time to remove the dynamite.

She and Bell had something in common, she realized. They were both unintentional participants in a murder. But as soon as she saw the parallel, a crucial difference leapt out at her. She hadn't told Fallon about Hunter with any expectation he'd act on the information, or any sense he could under the circumstances—a dying man in prison—but she had told him because he'd once taken justice into his own hands, as she'd desired to do with Hunter. Unlike Bell, then, she'd had murder in her heart. And if she were being honest, it was still there. She didn't feel much resistance to her legacy.

Something else occurred to her. The idea of killing Hunter and burying her in the cemetery had felt like a fantasy in its conception, and that's how she'd regarded it ever since. There were too many people around—Maria in the house, Reggie and Juan somewhere on the property, Sally returning at some point. But looked at from another angle, the feeling might have been an intuitive appraisal of the risk. Take the risk away and then what? Her uncertainty about the answer was the most damning thing of all.

She turned the car around and drove back through the shadows to the main road. By the time she reached it, an inner voice had begun defending her against her dark thoughts. The voice belonged to Jack, and she imagined him at the kitchen table across from her, speaking calmly and sensibly. *It was just a fantasy*, he would say. *The proof is you didn't act on it. The reason it disturbs you is that it's so out of character for you. But that can be explained too. It was a response to a unique set of factors, never to be repeated: disappointment over being fired, anger over the deaths of Steve and Rachel, fear for your loved ones, and frustration with a justice system that refused to take notice of Hunter. And the one who made it into a reality wasn't you; it was Fallon. He may have thought he was saving you from doing something rash, but unconsciously he wanted to justify his first crime in your eyes by entangling you in the second one. You're as much his victim as Ashley Hunter is.*

The weakness of this quite plausible defense was that she didn't believe it, and by the time she got home, her dark thoughts had prevailed. They'd even commandeered Yeats for their use. In "The Second Coming" she'd always identified with the falconer, the representative of order and restraint, but now she saw herself in the lawless falcon, spiraling away from the person she'd assumed she was.

Her moral shrinkage, or self-recognition, was a burden she longed to lighten by sharing it with someone. She wasn't able to do it with Jeff, although she told him about her conversations with Hunter and Fallon. Nor could she do it with Sally. The whole sordid business would distress her friend too much and taint her remaining years. It had to be Jack. In fact, she needed it to be Jack. She hoped and trusted he'd say the sort of things she'd imagined for him, not because they'd be any more persuasive coming from the real Jack, but because they'd signify his forbearing love. But there was an obstacle to confiding in him that loomed larger the more she considered it. In carrying the tale of Hunter's confession to Fallon instead of to him, and saying nothing about it later, not even after Fallon's burial, she'd committed a kind of emotional infidelity. She'd chosen Fallon over Jack because, when it came to Ashley Hunter, Fallon was her kindred spirit. It was a worse betrayal, it seemed to her, than sleeping with Steve Williams. She and Jack had a life together now, and this required above all an openness about the important things. She'd violated their lovers' compact, and she feared if she told him, it would drive a wedge between them.

Her reticence, however, created its own problems. Outwardly, they went on as before. She spent her days either working at the farm or reading college texts, with more emphasis on the latter as June swooned into July. Jack still made dinner even though she'd offered to take over the job, having more time than he. After dinner they read together on the sofa and watched a little TV; and after that, they sometimes made love. But Jack, ever observant, could see she was troubled, and finally asked if there was anything she'd like to talk about.

"No," she said. "Not much point. I'm sad about some things, as you know, but I'm trying to get on with it."

"Nothing else?" he persisted.

"Isn't that enough?" she said, more sharply than she'd intended.

Following this exchange, he became quieter and more tentative around her. She didn't fully appreciate the damage she'd done until they were awakened one night by a powerful storm. As they listened in the dark to the rain thundering against the roof and pummeling the windows, he said with such un-ironic desolateness that she wondered for a moment if he'd become unhinged, "It's the end of the world." Then he added, "That's what my mother always said when it rained like this."

He was slipping away from her. She remembered thinking at Steve Williams' funeral that love and work were what she had instead of faith. Now, having lost the work, she was pushing away Jack's love. But she still couldn't muster the courage to reveal her disloyalty. She doubled down on the college reading, trying to distract herself with nineteenth century American prose. It was a futile effort. Great literature isn't a diversion; one way or another, it leads back to reality. The Transcendentalists' faith in human potential reminded her of her spiritual impoverishment. She couldn't say with Emerson, *Let us advance on Chaos and the Dark*. Or with Thoreau: *The life in us is like the water in the river. It may rise this year higher than man has ever known it, and flood the parched uplands.* She preferred Hawthorne and Melville, whose flawed characters made her feel less alone in her misery. *Ah, Bartleby! Ah, humanity!* But in *The Scarlet Letter*, she came upon something that denied her even this thin comfort: *Be true! Be true! Be true! Show freely to the world, if not your worst, yet some trait whereby the worst may be inferred.* When she'd first read the novel last year, the passage hadn't seemed to apply to her. This time it struck home as a censure, and a challenge.

Chapter 25

LATE IN THE SUMMER JACK was asked to participate in a terrorism seminar at Quantico. The event was scheduled for a Saturday, and she saw him off with a mixture of sadness at the distance between them and relief they wouldn't be together all day, treating each other with what seemed increasingly the outward forms of intimacy, in place of intimacy itself. But as she was clearing the table of breakfast dishes, sadness got the upper hand. She stopped and sat down and put her hands in her head. The newspaper was spread out before her, and she stared idly at it until, for some reason, the date commanded her attention. August 11. Why did that seem significant? Then she remembered it was the day Steve and Shannon had planned to be married. A hard day for Shannon. And one that threw an unflattering light on herself. She had what Shannon had lost, the great thing, and out of fear and shame she was letting it die. She needed to find a way to keep it alive.

After some thought, she dressed and drove to the big hardware store in Parkerville. She bought two paint brushes, a roller set, and a gallon of paint, choosing from the apparently infinite shades of off-white, and by the time Jack returned home late in the afternoon, she'd painted their bedroom walls except for the edging around the ceiling.

He noticed the smell right away. "Have you been painting?" he said.

"I have. Come and take a look."

She led him to the bedroom and pointed to the jagged band of old beige near the ceiling. "My painting arm still won't reach that high," she said.

"I'll finish it up. But the rest looks nice."

"I didn't think I could go wrong with white. If we do the other rooms, though, we could choose bolder colors."

"Fire-engine red?" he said. "Hot pink?"

"Maybe not that bold."

"You know what I'd like to do," he said. "Get rid of the plaid wallpaper in the bathroom."

"We could start there."

On Sunday, having read up on the process, they went into Parkerville and got the necessary equipment—scorer, broad knives, extra sponges—and stripped the wallpaper together, Jack doing the upper areas and she the lower. The job was more difficult and time consuming than they'd anticipated. But it had its compensations. They worked at close quarters, casually brushing against each other, arms and thighs touching. They hadn't had sex in several weeks now, and the physical contact felt both sensual and comforting to her. Doing this, they were a couple again.

When they finished, he said, "Good thing it's such a small bathroom."

"Yeah," she said. "I was beginning to get nostalgic for the plaid."

He proposed they have some wine to celebrate their achievement, and she proposed the backyard swing as the place to drink it. Glasses in hand, they went out through the tiny porch and sat facing the woods, Jack rocking the swing slightly with his legs.

"Be nice to have a garden back here," she said.

"Flower or vegetable?" he said.

"Both. Probably too late for either one this year. But there's always next year."

He stopped rocking and looked at her. "I'm glad you think so," he said.

"Of course I do," she said. "I'm sorry I've been sort of withdrawn lately. I've been dealing with some things I haven't told you about."

He waited.

"You were right about Steve Williams' death. It affected me more than I let on. I slept with him once. It was after I'd walked out on you in that Manassas restaurant for trying to cure my insomnia. A few days later I helped him with a hit and run, and ended up spending the night at his place."

Jack silently took this in.

"It was the only time," she said. "My decision. He made me feel too old. Also, I thought he was shallow womanizer. A mistaken impression, as I learned later."

"Oh," Jack said, with a hint of disappointment.

"But the main reason was I'd fallen in love with you."

"Even though you weren't speaking to me."

"Right."

After a moment, he said, "You don't make me feel old. The opposite."

"Good." She put her hand on his arm. "The other thing on my mind, I'm not ready to talk about yet."

"Okay."

"No additional lovers, though."

"Well, one's plenty."

They sipped their wine and looked at the trees. It was late afternoon, and the gnats were becoming a nuisance. There was a sympathetic description of gnats in Keats's "To Autumn"—*a wailful choir* rising or sinking as the wind blew—but those gnats weren't bothering anybody. Soon she and Jack would have to retreat. Meanwhile, a bird was singing in the wood, a cardinal she thought. Four or five loud sharp notes, repeated each time with conviction. And the sun, sinking on their right, had emblazoned that side of the trees, turning the green into gold. She looked for the cardinal and saw far back in the inky shadows a greenish flicker. Firefly.

Jack leaned over and gave her a winey kiss on the lips.

She kissed him back.

Thanks as usual to my publisher Jeanne Johansen of High Tide Publications and my editor Narielle Living. Also, a special thanks to David Elder, who suggested I bring back the character Mike Fallon, to Mary Roberts for reading and commenting on the manuscript, and to New River Valley Writers Group for doing the same for several chapters.

Bonus 1

The first chapter of H. Scott Butler's book

Night Journey

A Cynthia Westbrook Mystery

Books in the Cynthia Westbrook Series

Night Journey

Voice From the Shadows

Falcon

Chapter 1

SHE SHOULD SEE HIM NOW, he thinks, as he examines his chiseled upper body, shiny with sweat, in the closet-door mirror. She always mocked him for being puny, and he was puny. When he got his first barbell set two years ago, he could barely lift 130 pounds. Now he does lifts of 200 pounds and overhead presses of 110. And he might even be further along if he trained at a well-equipped gym. But he's chosen to keep his muscularity a secret. Maybe he's being overly cautious, but it seems wise not to call attention to himself in any way, and since he has the sort of modest frame that turns ordinary clothing into a disguise, why not use this to his advantage? Besides, he's already achieved his strength goal.

He lies down on the exercise mat, raises his knees, and comes up slowly, focusing the work in his abs and counting to himself at the top of each sit-up. After a few minutes a faint whiff of his own sweat reminds him of the smell of the nursing home, that strong urinal tang in the stifling air. He remembers how it seemed to fume off the pale yellow, piss-colored walls. When he complained about it once to his mother, she called him an ungrateful little shit—little shit being the constant in her rebukes. But it was hard to feel gratitude for having to sit so many hours in the nursing-home lobby among the stinking, toothless old wrecks in their wheelchairs. Most of them were zombies, empty-eyed and

*open-mouthed, but there was always at least one with just enough brain left
to harass him with some crazy request repeated over and over. He would make
faces at them, not that it ever did any good, and when he could get away with it,
he'd escape by roaming the building. This wasn't much of an improvement over
sitting in the lobby; the smell was even worse beyond the double doors that led
to the main hallway. But occasionally he'd come across something of interest,
like the time he opened the door to a room and saw Elroy the janitor with an
old woman.*

*Elroy was a skinny little man with rabbit teeth and no chin. He had a
high-pitched giggle, and his country accent sounded like grunts and gargles.
Momma called him a white trash moron. But the Elroy he saw that day was
transformed. He'd pulled the old woman around to the side of her bed and
was vigorously thrusting his shirt-tail-covered buttocks between her bare legs.
She, meanwhile, her face hidden, was making low moaning noises like someone
trapped in a nightmare. At the time he was too young to fully comprehend
Elroy's purpose, but there was no mistaking his power and decisiveness.*

*He remembers another door-opening episode that happened a few years later,
when he could stay by himself after school. He was eager to tell his mother
about his perfect score on a math test, but she called to say she had a meeting
with Mr. Dent and hung up before he could give her his news. He ordered
pizza and paid for it with the coffee-canister money, as he was allowed to do in
the circumstances, finished his homework, watched some TV, and finally got in
bed around midnight. He was still awake, however, when he heard her in the
hall. She hated any interruption to her routines, so he gave her time to take a
bath and get ready for bed. Then he went down to her room. He could hear her
radio playing, but not wanting to wake her if she'd drifted off, he opened the
door quietly. She wasn't asleep, or in bed. She was sitting at her dressing table
brushing her hair, and she was naked except for a pair of pink panties. She
must have seen him in the mirror because she spun around with a scowl on her
face. At the sight of her breasts, his thing jerked in his pajamas, but it was
the only part of him capable of movement. He watched her leap up and march
toward him, her breasts jiggling. Her nipples were pink in pink circles. She
was gripping the hairbrush, and when she reached him, she hit him hard with
it in the crotch. As he doubled over, screaming and grabbing himself, she said,
"That will teach you to knock, you filthy-minded little shit."*

He realizes he's lost count of the sit-ups. He may have reached a hundred, but it's important to maintain a sense of discipline. That's how he's come so far so fast. He begins over, and when he's counted off a hundred, he rolls out the barbell and slides on extra discs for the dead lifts. Staring down at the bar, he feels a slight sense of disappointment.

He's put considerable effort into being able to do what he does—lift a woman weighing 120 or 130 who was still seizing from the shock of the stun gun, elbow open the popped trunk, toss her in, cuff and gag her, all in a few seconds time. But this achievement is only the means to an end, and the end, so far, hasn't quite lived up to his expectations. The women he selected had seemed so sure of themselves, so smugly in control of their lives. It's the main reason he picked them. His plan was to strip away their confidence bit by bit. He imagined them offering him money, promising they wouldn't say anything, telling him they knew he wasn't really like this, reminding him of the executioner's needle, treating him like the stupid little man they thought he was. He'd pretend to be affected by their words; he'd express remorse for what he was doing to them, though continuing to do it of course. And so it would take them some time to realize his complete mastery of them. But he wasn't allowed this pleasure. Once he had them in his power, they put up no resistance at all, unless you counted begging; their self-assurance vanished like a mirage. Not that he considers his time with them wasted. Far from it. The second stage, as he thinks of it, has its own pleasures, the main one being rooted in necessity: to keep them from turning into zombies, you have to dole out some hope and relief, which adds a certain psychological interest. But even so, he won't be satisfied until he's fulfilled his first-stage fantasy.

Ironically, the closest he's come, from the standpoint of encountering resistance, was in his initial, botched attempt at a kidnapping. Everything went wrong. As soon as the bitch saw his knife, she started screaming and pulling away, and he was forced to use it on her—only to discover that he was too weak to drag her out of sight. He had to jump in his car and drive off with the body in plain view. For months afterward he lived in fear of the police knocking on his door. Yet in retrospect that single deep slash was more thrilling than anything he's done since. Her trophy is the one that still excites him the most.

He does ten dead lifts. Then he carries his dumbbells over to the mirror and begins a set of curls, watching his biceps bulge, relax, bulge. She's out there somewhere, he thinks. The woman who'll cling to her sense of superiority until he's shown her it doesn't exist. This time he'll get it right.

Bonus 2

The first chapter of H. Scott Butler's book

Voice from the Shadows

A Cynthia Westbrook Mystery

Books in the Cynthia Westbrook Series

Night Journey

Voice From the Shadows

Falcon

Chapter 1

SHE WAS FLYING THROUGH DUSKY woods, swerving around the black boles, her naked feet barely touching the ground. A branch struck her in the face and flung her backward to the earth, where she lay curled in on herself, trying not to breathe. Then it came to her: she wasn't a child anymore. She struggled to rise and woke herself up, though not to the familiar darkness of her bedroom. The dim window curtains seemed too large, and a strip of light shone under the door, where the door shouldn't be.

"Cynthia?" a groggy voice said.

She remembered. She was in a motel room with Jack. They'd spent the afternoon cruising Belmont Bay in his motorboat and an unplanned evening making love for the first time.

"Sorry," she said. "Just a dream."

His hand found hers under the covers. He probably suspected she'd dreamed about her mother's murder, since she'd told him the story on the boat, and he was letting her know he was ready to listen. She wasn't used to such tact from a man. Her male colleagues in the sheriff's office generally favored bluntness underscored by profanity. It was their way of showing, she suspected, they could stand up to the ugly truth. But Jack, an FBI forensic psychologist, used his innate subtlety in facing the ugliest truths of all. His duties included talking to serial killers, and he'd once told her he'd learned to interview them as if asking about their television viewing habits.

"I dreamed I was running away from my mother's killer," she said. "It was basically a memory except for the end, when I realized I wasn't a kid. So, Dr. Slaughter, your interpretation?"

"Yours is the one that counts."

"Well, in that case, I think it sort of confirms a decision I've made."

"Oh?"

"I'd intended to tell you after our boat ride. One thing at a time. But I got distracted."

"I remember."

"You should. You did the distracting."

"What did you decide?"

"I'm going back to Alabama to look into my mother's murder."

"I see."

She sensed a reservation lurking in that neutral response, but she knew Jack was wary of commenting on her personal issues. The one time he'd done it, trying to help her overcome a bout of insomnia, she'd gotten angry and walked out on him. Nevertheless, his suggestion that a childhood trauma might be involved had changed everything. It had spurred her to tell a comparative stranger—the first person she'd ever told—about her mother, which had forced her to confront the past she'd become so adept at evading. This had not only cured her sleeping problem but also freed her to re-think and solve the case she was working on. All because of Jack's spurned advice.

"Care to elaborate?" she said. When he didn't answer right away, she added, "I promise not to get mad."

"When would you go?"

"Soon. Now that I've got the time." Her last case, the one Jack had helped her with, had created a media storm that she'd escaped by taking a leave of absence.

"I certainly understand why you'd want to do it," he said. "But you've just begun to deal with those painful memories. Processing them there, where they were created, could be very stressful."

"So you think I should wait?"

"For a little while."

"But I've already waited twenty-four years."

"What's another month or two, then?"

"Her killer could still be killing."

"Or he could be dead, or in prison for another crime."

"Jack, I know I'm still… processing. But I'm sure I can handle it."

"Feelings can creep up on you. They can own you before you realize it."

Getting a little angry in spite of herself, she remained objective enough to see she couldn't blame Jack. She'd asked for this. She propped herself on an elbow and trained her dark-adapted eyes on him. The residual gloom softened his sharp features, but the arch of his eyebrows still suggested a movie villain of the comic variety, as did the errant lock of hair jutting from his widow's peak. His hazel eyes, drained to pearl gray, stared warily up at her.

"I appreciate the advice," she said, "and I'll keep it in mind."

"Would you like me to go with you? I could try to wrangle—"

"Thanks," she interrupted, "but I'll be talking to small-town folks in an unofficial capacity. They might put up with me since I'm from there. But you they'd regard as an intruder."

"I wouldn't want to get in the way," he said doubtfully.

"You could still help, though, by giving me your thoughts on the killer."

He let out a barely audible sigh. "Okay. Tell me everything you remember."

His assent had the unexpected effect of making her balk. When she'd told him about the murder earlier, she'd stuck to the essential facts, but now she'd have to flesh them out, to put her mother's flesh into the story. She took a deep, silent breath, released it slowly, and said, "I was sitting on the back steps, listening to the cicadas in the woods. He jumped up from behind the gardenia bush next to the house. The strange thing was, I'd been wondering why the cicadas sang, and it was like he'd popped up to answer my question."

"Not so strange," Jack said. "It's hard to take in a sudden threat. Your mind resists it, tries to domesticate it. Can you describe him?"

"He looked to be in his twenties—at least from my nine-year-old's perspective. He might have been younger. He was white, medium build. He had brown hair and a nice face with light blue eyes. It was the eyes that scared me first. He looked at me the way a cat looks at a bird."

"What happened next?"

"He came rushing around the bush, with a piece of firewood raised over his head. I tried to yell, but nothing came out. The next thing I remember is lying in the dirt. My head hurt, and I guess I wanted my mother to look at it. I climbed the steps to the door, which was slightly ajar. I pushed on it, but it wouldn't budge. So I squeezed through the crack."

She stopped, having reached the unimaginable, the sight still sending shock waves through her life. Jack remained quiet.

"What was blocking the door," she forced herself to say, "was my mother's body. Her head was against it." She saw her mother's eyes, blank as stone. "Her hair was bloody. She was bloody all over. And she was naked except for her tube top, which had been pulled down to her middle. I said, 'Momma,' and the refrigerator door closed, and there he was, holding a can of beer. He said, 'You again,' and I spun around and pushed through the crack and ran. I didn't even think about it. I just did it. I ran into the woods, and I kept running until a branch hit me and knocked me down. Lying there I could hear him coming. He shouted that the woods were full of snakes, and he'd bet there were bears and bobcats too.

When this didn't scare me into the open, he said I'd hurt my head and my mother was worried about me. By then he was almost on top of me, and I shut my eyes. But suddenly he changed direction. He was furious now, calling me names, yelling if he had to find me I'd wish I was my mother. How long this went on, I don't know, but when I couldn't hear him anymore, it was dark."

Jack had turned toward her while she talked, and they lay facing each other. Beneath his villainous brows, his eyes shone with compassion. He let a few moments pass before saying, "You sure it was a piece of firewood he hit you with?"

"Pretty sure."

"Doesn't sound like something he would've brought along."

"There was a stack behind the bush."

"Okay. Now tell me about your mother's body. Did you see any wounds?"

"I just remember the blood."

"And you found her in the kitchen?"

"Yes."

"He could have stunned her with the firewood, and then, considering all the blood, shot or stabbed her. My guess is he used a knife."

Following Jack's lead, she said, "Maybe it was one of ours from the kitchen. Another weapon of opportunity like the firewood."

"And if that's the case, he didn't plan ahead; he acted impulsively. So it's possible he'd never killed before—a theory his youth would support. Did he seem drunk or high?"

She compared her memory to later experiences. "No."

"Where was your house? It must have been fairly isolated if he felt free to shout at you in the woods."

"We were eight miles from town, with nobody nearer to us than a mile or so."

"He might have just happened upon the house. But it seems

more likely he either knew your mother or saw her somewhere else and found out where she lived."

"She worked as a waitress at a diner in town. He could have seen her there."

"Suppose he did, and followed her home. How would he have known there was no other adult in the house, or one coming later?"

Washing the dishes, the bare tops of her shoulder blades moving like bird's wings, Momma said, "Just listen to those cicadas."

"The windows were open," Cynthia said. "He could have heard us talking over dinner, just the two of us." Strange and terrible to think of him spying on them like Satan in the garden. What would he have heard? Her mother asking about her day, as she always did. And since it was summer, Cynthia telling about her time at the Wades. Janice Wade, the other waitress at the diner, had kept her several days a week in the summers, and Cynthia would ride into town with her for the late afternoon switch off. But she could remember nothing of this precious last conversation with her mother except the washing-up part. She'd asked why the cicadas sang, and her mother had answered, whimsically it seemed to her now, "Maybe they just like having a sing-along."

"So we can't rule out his being a stranger," Jack said. "How was he dressed?"

"Dark slacks, maybe. A light-colored shirt."

"Were his clothes unusual in any way? Dirty, torn?"

"I don't think so."

"What else did you notice about him?"

She'd spent the last twenty-four years trying not to remember anything from that day or her life before it. She'd learned to shift her thoughts elsewhere, to lose herself in books. But the memories were still there, waiting to be called forth. She saw him again standing by the refrigerator. His forearms and shirt were smeared and dappled a bright arterial red.

"Nothing, except…"

"What?"

"Not relevant. In the kitchen, he was covered in blood."

Jack winced. This was hard on him too, she realized.

"Can you describe his voice?" he said. "Not so much the pitch as the other qualities."

It was something she hadn't thought of. "He didn't sound like us, exactly."

"Not Southern, you mean?"

"No, it wasn't that. His accent was... less hicky than ours. More like the doctor's."

"So, a different social background?"

"Maybe." She heard him in her mind. No double negatives or verb errors. No rural or working-class colloquialisms. And until rage had drowned it out, a kind of coldly ironic sensibility. "You again," he'd said, as if she were a pest he couldn't rid himself of. "Bears and bobcats," he'd shouted almost playfully in the woods. Lions and tigers, oh my.

Jack was silent for a while. "I don't have much for you," he said finally. "He may have been a first-time killer. And he may have occupied a higher rung on the social ladder than you and your mother. That's about it."

"No other thoughts?"

"I wish you'd put off going."

She leaned in to kiss him on the lips. The dawn light seeping into the room had restored the polished hazel of his eyes.

www.ingramcontent.com/pod-product-compliance
Lightning Source LLC
Chambersburg PA
CBHW070920130626
46555CB00001B/213